Ghost PILOT

by Gene Geyman

Illustrated by G. C. Pomeroy

Copyright ©2002 by Gene Geyman

Illustrations by G. C. Pomeroy

Published by Avian Ridge Books
34 Oak Hill Drive
Friday Harbor, WA 98250

All rights reserved. No part of this work may be reproduced or utilized in any form or by any means, electronic or mechanical including photocopying, recording, or by any information storage and retrieval system without written permission from the publisher, with the sole exception of brief passages quoted in a review or critical essay.

ISBN 0-9674369-2-3

Library of Congress Control Number: 2002102524

Printed in the U.S.A. by CreateSpace

For my husband, John

And with thanks to the
Glider Council of Seattle.

CHAPTER 1

By late afternoon, the weather had gone wild up on Loftsman's Hill, but A-K didn't care. 'Least, that's what he said.

"See, you need a bunch of wind, you wanna fly anything," he told his nephew. Kneeling, he added one more rubber band attaching the Condor's long wing to the fuselage. "Hey, Petey, you warm enough?"

"Yeah, m'okay," the seven-year old answered. He'd been rubbing his chapped hands together, but now he stopped. "So- now can I fly my plane, Uncle Andor?"

"Not yet. Wait a l'il bit for the wind to slow down. Hey, and don't call me Andor, remember ? It's 'A-K'. Neb'mind what the folks call me."

On the long, hot car trip, moving from Arizona out to the Coast here, he had determined to re-name himself. Back home, most of the teachers called him "Andy". His parents called him "Andor". Now, although he couldn't do much about his height— almost all his relatives were small—he wanted a tough name. A-K! Send out the message, he was no pushover.

Petey, ignoring his uncle's advice about the wind, picked up his dime store glider and began tossing it into the air again. After each hard landing, the heavy wind skiddered the plastic plane all over the hill but the little boy kept trying.

A-K pretended not to notice. Ignoring the dents in his knees from working on the rocky hill, he kept wrapping more and more rubber bands onto the plane's long fuselage.

Gonna get this plane in the air.

"Soon's as I get the Condor launched, you and me can have this big plane war," he promised his nephew.

Finally, the long red wing was secured. His plane, put together now, was huge: wingspan, alone, was almost long as a door. Getting up on stiff legs, A-K decided he'd give it a couple more minutes and let the wind drop off some.

First time he'd seen St. Clair from up this far.

Crummy lookin' town they'd moved to, in his opinion. Now where?—he squinted—oh yeah, the new school is that blah-colored building down there, next to the park. And, like, gimme a break, he thought, the whole downtown isn't more'n six blocks long—seven, if you counted that garden nursery, off a-ways.

Shoot, this place is nothin' like Tucson.

Shaking his head, his eyes followed the highway out of town. It disappeared into a forest of giant-sized trees—re-appeared in time to roll through the next place, Milltown, then popped out on the freeway again, aiming for Seattle.

"Listen, Petey, " he said, turning back to his nephew, "the Wright brothers didn't just hang around, waitin' for the perfect time." Puffs of steam came out of A-K's mouth with every word. "You know, at Kitty Hawk?"

"Uh huh, you already tol' me, Uncle Andor," the little boy said. "So, when're you gonna fly your plane, anyways?"

"Real soon! But, listen, you gotta call me 'A-K'. Get it? Nevermind the grownups—they can't 'member anything."

The seven-year old shrugged. "Yeah. Okay. But when're you gonna..."

"NOW! That's when," A-K shouted over the wind. With the motion of an outfielder throwing for home plate, he lobbed his red Condor straight into the wide-stretching air.

It turned out the paper-and-balsa plane flew even better than he'd hoped. The glider shot out from the hill until the furious wind grabbed it and carried it upwards.

Barely breathing, he watched the graceful ship soar. Almost two weeks he'd been working on the thing. Started just a few days after they'd moved out here to St. Clair.

"Ya-ay!" Petey shouted. "It works!"

Both boys stood, top of the hill, transfixed. Behind the red glider, the chrome sky was like a time-lapse movie: high, rollicking clouds banged themselves apart; briefly, pale yellow light streamed down on them. Then the clouds swirled together again, blotting out the sun.

"Man-oh-man, it's really cruisin' !" A-K whispered. Seemed like right after he said that, though, his balsa plane did a 180 . Stalling, the big model nosed up for a brave second, then was whipped over on its side by an erratic gust of wind. Kamakasi-like, it dove straight for the ground.

Immediately Petey took off right down the hill, his spindly arms outstretched. "Gettin' it for ya," he hollered over his shoulder. "Don' worry. I'll get it!"

A-K squinched his eyes tight a second. Then he spurted right after his nephew.

But it was too late: the big Condor had smashed down onto the packed dirt of Loftman's Hill.

Looked like kindling, parts of it.

"Got busted," Petey croaked after a minute. "Jus' what Grandpa said'ud happen."

"Hah-hh-a," A-K exhaled. "Crap!" He picked up a couple pieces of the broken wing; limply attempted to heft some of it back in place, then quit. Naw, no use, 'till he got home.

Red tissue paper, torn loose at the breaks, flapped in the wind. On the inside, you could still see some of the unbroken struts. Intricate as a bee hive. Or a cathedral.

"Stupid damn dumb day!" he shouted. He felt a rumble of sobs at the base of his throat but choked them down. Instead, he kicked viciously at a large, half-buried stone. The rock didn't budge and his foot felt about killed.

The pain was a relief.

"Lookit, Petey," A-K got out, gathering up scattered pieces of the glider, "just lem'me pick up my junk an' you get your plane. Okay? We gotta go home."

For once, Peter kept his mouth shut.

Three blocks away from Loftman's Hill, the two boys heard a droning noise overhead. Automatically, A-K tipped his head up to look. Directly above them was a white floatplane with little pontoons all snug underneath. A bright flash of sun bounced off its wings.

Yeah, the wind's knockin' him around, too, A-K thought. But 'least the pilot's doin' it. You can't jus' sit around waitin' for perfect weather, no sir!

Briefly comforted, he lowered his eyes, and that's when he saw a bunch of kids. Hard not to notice them.

One of them, this bruiser-type guy in a green and white letterman's jacket, looked familiar. Yeah, A-K remembered seeing him at the new school, always whooping it up with his show-off friends.

Right now, it looked like the three guys were playing this dumb game of knock-each-other off-the-curb. The two girls pretended to ignore them. Facing each other, they chatted and smoothed out their wind-blown hair with polished fingernails.

The back of A-K's neck started burning, as if the biggest zits in America had just popped out on him. The whole bunch of them—you could tell by their clothes—were probably like the top kids.

"Hey, how come we're goin 'so fast," his nephew complained. He half-ran, half-hopped, trying to keep up with his uncle's speedy pace.

"Neb'mind, Petey. Jus' hustle." A-K clenched his teeth, thinking, oh man, gotta get past them fast. Huddling the plane wreckage up against his chest with both arms, he moved so fast it was almost running. It didn't work, though.

The letterman guy suddenly spotted A-K and the nephew. Looking around to make sure he had an audience, the big kid sang out, "Up in the sky, junior bird-men, up in the air, fairy's fly..."

"Give it a rest, will ya?" A-K muttered. His heart was near busting out of his shirt but he tried to look totally tough.

Someone—it was the dark-haired girl —said, "Oh, c'mon, Marko, leave them alone."

That Marko shut up, instantly. Still—probably blaming the stranger for getting him into trouble, the guy flashed A-K a slit-eyed look, like—okay, buddy, I'm not gonna forget this. It was like a telegram: You just made me look bad.

Then, re-arranging his face—you could see the letterman guy really liked that one girl—he pasted on a fake smile. Turning back to his friends, he shrugged, like—well, now's I got rid of the rif-raff, everything's fine again.

When they got close to home Petey ventured, "Uncle Andy, you gimme fifty cents, I'll tell ya what my folks are gonna give you for your birthday."

A-K was still so bummed out he couldn't even fake a smile. "Just forget it, Peter-Peter," he said wearily. "I like surprises." Also, he figured if he waited a little longer, his nephew wouldn't be able to stand it and would tell him for free.

The trouble was, with St. Clair being such a small town and all, the boys arrived home too soon for that to work.

When they arrived at the modest house A-K's parents had just bought, he hesitated. No cars out in front but that didn't mean anything. His brother and sister-in-law usually just walked over. The folks parked in back. Probably everybody was there, already, because of the party.

Well, actually – his party.

Now, holding the plane as if it were a wounded bird, he marched in the front door. Petey—maybe expecting trouble—sort of tiptoed in behind him.

Bad luck: the minute A-K walked in he could hear the mournful strains of one of Dad's violin tapes playing on the recorder. Cigarette smoke hung in the air, so the folks had been there a while. Waiting for the birthday boy.

No chance of sneaking up to his room before the family spotted him.

Four grown-up Kerzaks sat at the end of the living room, playing cards. Three of them smiled at the boys as A-K tried to hustle past the stucco archway. But no smiles from his father. Like a laser beam, Victor Kerzak's narrow-eyed stare landed on the smashed-up plane.

"Ja, Andor, like I tol' you," he said in his flat voice. "Reminds me uf Cub Scouts."

Sure, how could A-K forget ? When he was ten and a half, back in Tucson, he'd worked endless days on a chunk of balsa wood, planning to enter a Pinewood Derby Contest. Just before the race—and in spite of Dad's stern advice: "Stop, now!", he'd kept on tinkering. At the very last minute, A-K'd attached one more tiny piece of lead under the body of the model, with a blob of Super Glue. Hoped just that extra piece would increase the race car's speed, and he might win.

But when he got to the contest building, one of the officials—seemed like a decent guy—had to tell him the car's weight was over the limit. Just barely, but that was enough. A-K had knocked himself out of the race.

Wasn't quite the same deal, but he knew what Dad meant. You're always so impatient. Never do things right.

There was a painful silence in the warm, smoky room. Then his older brother, Josef, swiped a hand over his lion-colored hair—same hair as A-K had, only Josef didn't have as much. "Pretty unusual, this much wind in September," the brother offered. "When I got up this morning, weather seemed like it was going to be a great day. Sure changed in a hurry."

A-K knew Josef was trying to bail him out but he wasn't entirely grateful. Sometimes it bugged him that his grown-up brother tried to be such a good guy all the time. Hard to believe Petey was his kid.

"Now, family," his mother said, right after, "how about playing a nice game of Monopoly? It'd be fun, with all of us here." Always, those hopeful blue eyes.

"Nope, not for me, Mom, but thanks." A-K headed for the stairs. "Maybe Peter."

His father's flat voice chased after him. "Don' get lost up zere. Andor. Your mother's been vorking all day on your birthday dinner."

As if A-K didn't know.

Sure, he thought. *Thanks for telling me, Dad.* "O-kay, I'll be back down in ten minutes," he called. "Just got to get my — act together, first."

CHAPTER 2

Well, you've gotta hand it to Hungarians, A-K thought, coming down a half hour later. They sure know how to put on a party.

The whole house smelled like a delicatessen – the air, warm and breathy, was full of spice smells. Wine for the grownups, gingerale for the kids. A lot of laughing, a lot of talk.

His birthday dinner featured all his favorites, too – chicken paprika, creamy spazle noodles, the deep-fried langos bread they all loved. Sweet and sour cabbage salad. At the end, though, Mom did not serve up one of her famous tortes. Instead, at her younger son's request, she'd cooked up a tall, American-style cake – loaded with thick chocolate frosting, fourteen blue candles and three white inches of "Andor" piped across the top.

His brother's wife, Phoebe, a red-faced woman who was a social worker, thumped him on the back after he'd sat down next to her. It had been the only place left.

"So! How's it feel to be a big-ol' teen-ager, Andy?"

"Okay, I guess", he said, staring at the tablecloth.

"Old enough to get a part-time job, don'cha think?" Phoebe nudged him playfully, probably aiming for his arm. Where she got him, though, was in the ribs.

Irritated, A-K thought of telling her about the paper route he'd had for three years back in Tucson, but – why bother? She didn't listen to other people, she just gave advice.

Anyway, he knew his aunt meant he was old enough to start working at the dry cleaners. Just thinking about it made him start jittering his foot.

"Listen, Mom," he called across the table, "that was a real great dinner! Lotta work for you."

"You're welcome," she said, pleased.

Now, in a strained voice the family recognized as holding back much emotion, his father took over. With his right hand over his chest, a gesture that almost drove A-K up the wall, Dad began by saying how much it meant to him to be living here in this "land of freedom". Oh man, A-K thought, even on my birthday! I must'a heard this spiel ten million times.

"Just because zose hot shot business guys back in Tucson bought up our whole block for that shopping mall, leafing us high and *dry*... " His father waited several seconds for the family to laugh at the joke – which, dutifully, the grownups did – "vell, now look vot has happen: bought us a new dry cleaners, and here ve all are, living in the same place of St. Clair, Vashington!"

"Hey, Dad," Joseph called from his end of the table. "We're real glad ourselves!"

My big brother probably means it, too, A-K thought. Nice guy. Too nice, maybe.

"And also, Mother Kerzak," Phoebe stuck in, "if sometimes at night? Well, 'babysitting' in this town is real expensive, so maybe, if you'd ever would want to... " But she shut up when her husband frowned at her.

Oblivious, Mom re-pinned several strands of her silvery-blond hair back into the bun on top of her head. Her kind, round face was wistful like a girl's.

A-K sighed and stared up at the ceiling. Kind of unfair. It was turning out to be a grownup's party. Sure would be different if he were back in Arizona right now. He and his friends would've polished off the cake, and would be messin' around outside this very minute, havin' fun.

He swallowed hard, remembering, then sat up straight and watched Dad's fine-boned hands as they pantomimed his feelings.

"First, we mus' thank Josef and Phoebe for calling us on the long distance," his gray-haired father began. "For letting us know the Dry Rite Cleaners vas for sale."

He looked emotional, his high pale forehead creased with seriousness. "So! I haf come from – hardship." Viktor Kerzak's eyes slid over to his wife, then dodged away. "But now, it is oh-fer."

Gimme a break, A-K thought. You've been in America over forty years. What's that saying: The Hungarian is happy, no, is happiest in tears.

"The main thing is, with such a family as I haf," his father finished up, "I know the customers vill be coming, nefer'mine about that dry cleaners in Milltown. You'll see."

Phoebe reached out and squeezed Mom's hand. Petey fake-dropped his napkin, then scooted his chair over close to his uncle.

Their former shop partners in Tuscon, the Zaleys, had sent A-K a large picture book, with slick, beautiful pages showing photographs of fighting planes from all over the world. That was the first present.   Bet that's the best one, too, he thought. Zaleys always know what I want.

Next, his father got up and, without ceremony, plunked a large wrapped-up box down in front of him. Oh, man, oh please, A-K thought, hope it's a neat sweater, or maybe a denim work shirt. Something like what the guys wear around here.

Yanking away the ribbons first, then all the whispery tissue paper, he found himself staring at a heavy, dark-brown corduroy jacket inside the box.

"A brand new one for school," Mom told him proudly. "And I've sewn your name in it already!"

Without changing his expression, A-K instantly saw that the coat with the big, square shoulder pads and four leather buttons was expensive and – wrong. A style meant for grownups, not for kids. Here in St. Clair, he'd already noticed the guys wore mainly ski jackets made out of that wet-looking material, or the fleecy Northwest kind of polar stuff.

"Listen, thanks, Mom and Dad." A-K said after a careful minute. "I bet it's gonna be real warm."

"Also, Andy," Phoebe chimed in, "it's good enough so you can wear it to church."

Because he felt almost as bad for his clueless parents as he did for himself, he popped up out of his chair, gave his mother a kiss on her soft cheek, then leaned over and tried an awkward over-the-shoulder hug to his bony father.

"Yeah, when it gets cold around here... bet it'll be nice and um, heavy," he said.

Here was the best thing: Unexpectedly, his shy, grown-up brother gave A-K twenty-five beautiful magnificent dollars in a long white envelope – two crisp tens and a five. Probably Joseph felt sorry for him as a "new kid" and not having any friends right now, but neb'mind. Twenty-five bucks – All RIGHT!

Instantly Petey fixed his blue eyes on him. Sure, A-K knew. Behind that innocent face, ol' Peter-Peter was calculating how he could help his uncle spend the money. Well, that li'l guy's just outta luck, he decided. This dumb place has nothin' but lousy weather and a buncha mean kids. Got no friends, the new school is gonna be gross and I know my relatives s'pect me to help out at the new cleaners, just like my big brother did at the other one.

For a minute he almost couldn't breathe. He imagined he might keel right over, probably comin' down with something like – asthma? (Exactly what *is* asthma, he wondered). But the tightness or whatever it was went away.

A-K swallowed hard. Wish I could jus' take off and head back to Tucson. Bet the folks wouldn't even be sorry. I know the Zaleys would take me in. They like me. I could pretend I was their grandson.

'Cept, you really can't get very far on twenty five dollars. Never mind. What I'm gonna do is spend that check on my self. Every damn cent.

CHAPTER 3

Two days later, A-K sat with his eyes resting on Miss Olney in homeroom English. The tall, earnest teacher glanced at the new boy from time to time, flattered at his rapt attention.

Truth was, though, he barely heard a word she said.

Right now he was imagining himself flying an old WW II P-51 fighter plane, like the one he'd just seen on a TV movie. Flying high at three hundred and fifty miles per hour, he flew escort for a bomber raid. Thin white clouds streamed past the cockpit.

Heading straight at them – the dreaded ME-l09s! As the enemy fighters drilled through the short distance between themselves and the Yanks, their machine guns started to...

A-K jumped, startled at the last bell of the school day. He glanced around as the class, suddenly full of energy, plowed toward the door. Naw, nobody noticed: Andy Kerzak, the invisible man.

Once outside though, he heard somebody holler, "Hey, man!" Wheeling his bike toward the rain-slicked street, he whipped around with a hopeful grin. Finally, *maybe,* somebody'd noticed the new guy.

Wrong move: that friendly voice wasn't meant for him at all. Even worse, as he'd veered his bike around, he ran directly into the person next to him.

"Hey – ow, STOP," exclaimed a girl's startled voice.

"Aah-hh," A-K groaned, barely able to meet her eyes. "Sorry!

I gotta be the biggest klutz in the world. Are you killed?"

"Well, no. Not quite," the surprised girl said. She leaned down and rubbed the back of one leg, then gave him a tentative smile. "Anyway, it was my fault too, trying to catch a friend 'fore the bus takes off."

Man, was she ever pretty! She had kind of a pixie face, with wide-set green eyes and long, dark hair. Suddenly he remembered – she was one of the girls hanging out with those kids on that corner, the one who didn't make fun of him.

He knew her name by now too, Tina Beckman. Everybody wanted to talk to her in the halls, seemed like. Real popular. Figured she wasn't more than an inch taller than he was, either.

A-K clunked his bike down on the wet curb. Fairly sure half the school was staring at them, he scrunched down and helped pick up the two Bic pens and a wet gray folder she'd dropped, along with sheets and sheets of binder paper, covered now with blue, melting lines.

Out on the rainy sidewalk, kids waiting for the school bus started calling things like, "Oo-oo, *Ti-na* ! Better call an *am*-bulance."

If that wasn't bad enough, now somebody familar-looking ... oh man, it was that hulky guy from last weekend – leaned out of the window of a parked jeep and hollered, "HEY, folks, read all about it! Reporter smashed by stoned biker!"

"Ignore him," that Tina said calmly. "It's just Mark McCallister, showing off again."

"Well, you didn't – sprain anything, I hope?

"No. Thanks, I'm fine. It's just these notes..."

She put the driest papers back into the folder, looked at several others and just left them out on top.

"So, you must be the new guy?"

Nodding, he looked everywhere but at her. She was so nice, he was embarrassed to meet her eyes.

A little smile started curling at the corners of Tina's mouth as she studied him. A-K, still looking past her, was fairly sure how she saw him: the sandy-colored hair, cut short and kind of uneven. A lot of bones showing in his face, same as his dad's, the tipped-up nose. Okay, foreign-looking, and he knew it.

"You know, I'm sure I've seen you some place before," Tina mused. Then she laughed at herself. "Sounds like a line doesn't it?"

He managed a fake laugh. No way did he want to remind her of that gross scene on the way home last week. What's that thing he'd heard one time? Oh yeah: "The silent man is never thought a fool."

Shrugging, he just smiled.

"Wait a minute. I remember!" The girl suddenly nodded to herself. "Last Saturday, weren't you carrying pieces of this big plane for some little kid?"

"Uh, yeah. Right." He started to leave it that way, but then his pride took over. "Only, the busted plane? Well, see – actually, it's mine. Gonna repair it this weekend."

"Great!" she said, her face lighting up. "I felt real sorry, seeing it all smashed up. Bet you worked on it a long time."

Sorry? Before he could figure why a girl like her would even care, a tall, cross-looking sophomore shoved past them, and thumped herself into the jeep. She had the same uppity look as the driver, like: Move aside, world. We are important! Then, right after that, the McCallister guy peeled out, leaving plenty of exhaust around, and then the school bus came roaring in.

Tina glanced at the bus, but didn't head off for it yet. "Both my brothers built model airplanes when they were still around," she told him. "And they were always having crashes."

He nodded in agreement. Bad deal, crashes.

"Guess you've been out to the airport, right?"

"Uh, no. My father brought us over by car. Route 66. You know, like the song?"

"No, wait," she said, not picking up on his attempt at a joke. "I didn't mean when you moved here. See, there's this little airfield like, maybe an hour out of town? Forty-five minutes? Anyway, one end's totally for sailplanes and gliders. Wasn't that what you were carrying the other day, a glider?"

Catching his breath, A-K nodded.

"Thought so," she went on. "Well, and see, the other end's for power planes – the single engine ones. Actually, I think they even keep some ultralites out there."

She sure seems interested in this stuff, he thought. Wonder how come...

As if reading his mind, she volunteered, "Brad, my big brother, when he was still home? That's where he learned to fly. Mom and I used to go out and watch him sometimes. Started flying lessons when he was just twelve years old."

TWELVE? No way. Shaking his head, A-K waited for her to tell him it was a joke.

"I mean it! And if you can pass the test, take the lessons and do okay, a person can get a student glider license at sixteen. Anyway, my brother did."

"For real?"

"No kidding." As if she were just waiting for his answer, Tina spanked some of the rain off of the top of her head, but didn't leave. She shifted the wet binder to her other hand, instead.

"Uh, so where'd you say this place is, exactly?"

"Well, look," she said, glancing at the almost-full school bus now, "first you take the overpass out of town. Except, instead of winding onto the freeway for Seattle, you just keep going straight east, maybe four or five miles. There's this sign on the left saying 'Gliderport'. Have to watch for it, though. Sign's real small."

"Zat right?" He swallowed several times in a dry throat. "Well, maybe I oughta check the place out sometime."

"Really should, yeah. So, when are you?"

"Uh, I guess this – afternoon. Today!" Surprised himself to hear it.

"Great! Go for it." Tina watched the yellow bus as it maneuvered out of the driveway, leaving a smelly trail of dark exhaust behind itself. "Well," she said, "I just missed my friend, but I'll call her tonight. Anyway, I will be on time to interview the new Vice Principal right now."

The impish girl started off, then turned back. "Oh, hey, I'm

Tina Beckman. Forgot to ask you, what's your name?"

Ever since he'd changed it on the trip over to this new town, the first time was always a hassle. "A-K," he said in a low voice.

"What? Sorry, I didn't get – tell me again... ?"

"A-K," he repeated stubbornly. "Alias, Andy Kerzak. And, um, jus' so you get to know my whole life story? My legal name's Andor."

Since she hadn't taken off yet, and he was lonely and she was especially cute, A-K went on in a rush: "See, I got named after a grandfather who got killed overseas. My dad's father Andor, he was like this war hero? Don' know much about him, though. My folks, they can't even stand to talk about whatever happened."

A flicker of pain crossed the small girl's face. "That's so sad... Well, anyway, hope you like it here," she said in a slightly higher voice. "Caio." Tina hurried back into the school building.

Naw, shouldn't have told her 'bout that stuff, he thought, pushing his bike into the street. Didn't mean it to go that way. Bet she thinks I'm a real dork.

CHAPTER 4

When A-K finally got out to the field, he saw that her directions were right-on, and, except for dodging a couple puddle splashing logger's trucks, the traffic hadn't been all that bad. He felt like the trip hadn't taken him more than forty minutes.

Anyway, after being a paper boy back in Tucson, riding out here three or four miles didn't feel all that long.

But the place was a disappointment. All the "famous" gliderport *was*, was nothin' but a single grass runway stretched out across a couple of po-dunk fields. Tall poplars were lined up

like pencils alongside a huge aluminum hangar down there at the far end. Must be for those power planes she'd mentioned.

Sure, that place looked pretty official, down there. But up here, all there was was this beat-up old trailer and a scattering of metal sheds around, most of them gone rusty. An old Mustang parked here in the lot. Across from the grassy runway, fenced in from the gliderport, a bunch of slow-walking cows wandered around.

Shoot, he thought, this is the boonies... one pure nothin'. How come that Tina – well, she probably didn't know much about planes. It was her brother who was the flyer, she'd said.

Back in Tucson, the little airport near his house was at least ten times as big as this one. It had neat, clipped grass and a big adobe building with couches and tables on the first floor. Great doughnuts. And, they never cared how old you were; you could just sit in there and listen to pilot stories long as you wanted to.

Those single-engine planes could take take off and land, almost eleven months of the year. Once in a while, a twin even cruised in.

While, here – hey, STOP, he ordered himself. Remember? That girl said they teach kids how to fly out here. Not just grownups. Kids!

In the gray, dissolving day, A-K resolved to at least give the place a chance. After riding out all this way, might as well see what's up, he thought.

Taped up on one of the trailer's smudgy windows was a hand-made sign listing prices of tows, sight-seeing rides and lessons. The message, "Glider Lesson – $36.00" jumped out at him.

At the bottom of the sign, in strong, forward-slanted writing, was the message, "See Pat Grogan, Mgr."

O-kay, he told himself, nothin' lost, nothin' gets ya anywheres, or however that saying goes. After taking a deep breath, the slight boy tapped on the trailer's door. Not getting a response he went ahead and gingerly pushed it open. Directly in front of him sat a middle-aged man with sparse red hair and a nose like a parrot.

The man looked up abruptly from a book he was reading. He didn't look all that friendly. A-K was tempted to turn right around and leave. But he didn't.

"Well, you're a brave soul," the man commented, putting a marker in the book. "Most folks are 'fraid they'll melt in this kind of weather. But not you, huh?"

A-K yanked his shoulders back, trying to look like a brave soul "No sir, little rain doesn't bother me. See, what I want is, well, no, wait: Please, are you Mr. Grogan?"

"All depends. Are you a bill collector?" Straight-faced, the chubby man tipped back in his plastic-covered chair.

"Me ? Oh no, sir."

"Well, good. And I certainly hope you're not one of those Boy Scouts tryin' to sell me a box of cookies. Are you?"

"No way!" Actually, A-K was pretty sure it was the *Girl* Scouts who sold cookies but decided it wasn't too cool to correct him.

"Great, glad to hear it. So what can I do for you, son?" Now the man looked more friendly.

"Uh, sir?" He swallowed again. "I was jus' wondering if you'd ever gimme, give me, like, a glider lesson? See, I'm fourteen now, and-I-got-the-money..."

"Fourteen, huh?" Mr. Grogan said, bringing the tipped chair down onto the metal floor with a sharp clunk. "And you just robbed a bank, right?"

Trying to get in on the joke, A-K attempted, "Uh, no, sir. See, the bank was – it closed too early, so I couldn't pull it off."

"Ahh, lucky for them! Well, yes, I could probaby give you a lesson, sometime. Fourteen's old enough. But to start with, you'd need an adult's permission, in writing. Also, information 'bout your eyesight, health – a lot of stuff." Smiling, the manager reached around and rubbed the back of his neck. "Think you could get all that?"

Straight-faced, A-K nodded, not at all sure he could.

"Yes? Okay. So, lemme try an' find some of the things we need. Wasn't expecting anybody coming out, day like this..."

The manager pushed a white paper bag across the desk. "May as well have a doughnut, while I'm – yeah, go on and help yourself, son. I'll be looking for the forms we need."

Nodding thanks, A-K took one of the doughnuts and then sat down on the nearest seat. Too wired to eat, he started checking the place out.

Along the two long sides of the trailer were eight or nine of the gray cracked-leather seats, like the one he was sitting on. Must be old bus seats. The walls were bare metal, as if the insulation had been yanked off for some reason. Could'a just fallen off out of old age he thought.

A bunch of black and white plane photographs were pasted

up behind the manager's desk. Huge orange roses, biggest he'd ever seen, showed off in a tall brass vase on the desk. Down at the far end, there was an oil heater blasting away. Little hard to breathe in here, he thought, unzipping his jacket, but, thinking of their Tucson partners – remembered, ol' people' like plenty of heat.

"O-kay, now: a few little items we need to discuss 'fore we talk about a lesson," Mr. Grogan said, once he'd found the right papers. "First off – need your name and address, date of birth, all that stuff."

Holding his now-sticky doughnut in both hands, A-K told him what he wanted and the manager scribbled it all down. After staring at the note pad a minute, the man glanced up. "Kerzak, huh? Heard that name before but can't quite, place it." Lifting his eyebrows, he added, "You're not a politician or anything, are ya? Or a criminal?"

By now he realized the manager liked to joke around. He shook his head. "No sir. Not in this State, anyway."

Bet how Mr. Grogan knew his last name was because of Josef. With his working at the local hardware store, probably most everybody knew who he was. But A-K didn't want to start out that way – to be known as somebody's kid brother.

The manager rubbed his exceptional nose a few seconds, then went on cheerfully. "Okay. Next question. Can you get a parent or guardian to sign a permission slip for you?"

A-K skipped a breath. He knew his father would probably hit the roof when he heard about it. "VOT? Me sign permission for a glider lesson?" he'd say. "Better I should drop dead. Hah! Zose things are for rich people, not the likes of us."

But Dad doesn't know everything, A-K thought. Maybe I'll just fill the whole thing out myself. Forge the signature. 'Less I go back to delivering papers again, it's gonna be a while 'fore I get this much money again.

"Yes, sir," he said. "I'll get it signed." Later on, he'd figure out how. Maybe his big brother? Or the Zaleys, back in Tucson...

"And I can pay in cash. Don't haf to worry about that." The

birthday present, plus the twenty dollars from his paper boy savings from Tucson.

Mr. Grogan put his pencil down and started massaging the back of his thick neck. The man had a lot of laugh lines around his eyes, A-K thought, sneaking looks at him. Seemed like the ol' guy was pretty good friends with himself.

"Sounds fine. You get that signature and we're on. Now let's hear 'bout you? What's your story?"

It was A-K's nature to respond to friendliness with total abandon. Soon he was describing how it had been the last three months, about their Arizona partners retiring, the difficult move, Dad's buying the new business here. And also, the surprise birthday check.

"You a model builder?" Mr. Grogan asked, when A-K had wound down.

"Yes, sir." At least in here, that didn't make him sound like such a nerd. "In fact, you should'a seen the models I had to give away when we left Tucson. It was gross." Lucky for his friend Chub, though.

"Understand. Same with me, growing up. Parents always called me 'plane crazy'. Well, what you're tellin' me is, you'd like just one lesson, to see what soaring's all about. Right?"

"Right!" Energized, the boy moved out to the edge of the sagging chair.

"And I guess you'll be working part-time for your family, will you?"

The question took A-K off guard. In Tucson, his parents had co-owned the business with the Zaleys, their Hungarian partners. Back there, the folks hadn't needed him in the shop. Also, he'd been busy with his paper route, delivering and collecting. But now...

"Not quite sure, sir."

Nodding amiably, the manager flipped open a black date book on the desk. "Okay. Well, look's like I can give you a lesson this coming Saturday. 'Less there's rain, how 'bout ten o'clock in the morning?"

"Oh yes, sir, great. Terrific! I'll be here."

"Look forward to it. Oh, and I want to loan you something, if I can find it here..." The manager heaved himself out of his desk chair and began prowling through a shelf above his desk. "Trouble is, I keep lendin' out my books and... oh yeah, here it is – *A History of Sailplanes*. You might like to read it."

"Yes'sir, I will. And thanks a lot. Unless there's a big storm goin' on, I'll be here. Saturday – at ten oh oh."

"Sounds good," Mr. Grogan said. "And, of course, bein' as how you're a minor, when you come back, don't forget, you need a signed permission slip from at least one of your parents."

Permission slip ? A-K's face didn't change, but inside he hardened up. Saturday, I'll be back here with the note – even if I have to write it myself.

CHAPTER 5

In the morning, A-K kept his eyes closed a while longer, trying to hold onto the dream he'd had. In his sleep, he was still living back in Tucson. The air had felt like gingerale and he and his best friend were hurling planes up at the sun, exchanging insults, each of them trying to beat out the other guy for distance. And now, suddenly awake...he remembered.

Saturday! My flying lesson!

Now how 'bout the weather? The minute he poked his head out the window, a small cloud of birds rose up from the lawn and settled lightly on the next door neighbor's roof. Behind them, a blue and yellow sky.

Per-fec-to!

Except, wait a minute: had his father signed the slip? Thursday night, when A-K asked him for permission, their "little talk" ended up sounding like one of those radio operas the folks played on the weekends.

"People like us can't afford zoze things," his father had announced, and "ever-day, Andor, pick up the paper und you read 'bout another plane crash." He'd finished up by saying, "Start off life as a playboy, you vill end up in the bread lines. Jus' how it happens!"

"No wait, Dad," A-K said, stepping right up next to him. "How 'bout listening to my side, okay? See, I've been studyin' up on sailplanes a whole lot and..."

"Vot? First you're talking about gliders. Now it's sailplanes? What ist next, please? Jumbo jets?"

"No, Dad, I'm serious. C'mon, can I just please finish my sentence?"

His agitated father glared at him a second, then turned his hands upside down. "Ja, sure. So talk."

"Well see, for one thing, gliders and sailplanes, they're a lot the same. Mainly, it's jus' that sailplanes are bigger." 'Higher performance' it said in the books. 'Faster'. But no use getting into that right now.

Immediately his dad shook his head, bent forward, no doubt getting ready for another onslaught,

"But see, the main thing is," A-K went on quickly, "I read in these books, Hungarian pilots were totally famous in World War II. 'Bout the way they flew gliders back behind the enemy lines? And, you know, nobody could stop 'em!"

He had read every word in Mr. Grogan's loaner book.

"Vell—of course!" the excitable man said, backing off a little. "All the vorld knows that. But vot's that got to do vith you?"

"Dad," he said, trying for calm, "I'm Hungarian myself, y'know. And I never heard of those pilots ending up like 'play-boys'. Never. What I heard was—they were heroes!"

Taken aback, his father frowned, looking uncertain. Seeing that, A-K added, "An' also, it's only for the one time, you know. My birthday present. Almost all the money's from Josef"

Fingering his salt and pepper mustache, Victor Kerzak murmured, "Saturday, huh? Vell, let me talk over vis your mother."

Now, as A-K raced down the steps shirtless and shoeless, he thought—I'll forge that signature if I have to. I *will*.

The kitchen was quiet; too early for the folks to be up yet. 5:47 on the stove clock. He wondered if Dad had actually meant to sign the form but had forgotten. HOLY TOLEDO, there it is!

He grabbed up the slip next to the blue sugar bowl where it had been propped. Bee-*u*-tee-ful: there was Dad's full name, signed in his spidery, old-world handwriting.

So how come he ended up doin' it? Mom's influence? A-K figured he'd probably never know. Even though his father made such a racket about little things, the big stuff he never explained.

Could'a been his big brother, talked Dad into signing...

For breakfast, A-K smeared peanut butter on several of his mother's chocolate chip cookies, ate them fast, then washed everything down with a can of Pepsi. Feeling guilty, he reached into the fruit bowl and also ate two purple grapes, probably unwashed, but Mom wouldn't know.

In the living room he watched several minutes of an old Steve Martin movie on television, then switched it off. Naw, this wasn't one of the funny ones.

Why wait around? Might as well head out to the airport even if it was a little early. Hang around here much longer, Dad might wake up and say he'd changed his mind. It'd be just like him, too.

Whizzing down Main Street on his bike, A-K sneaked a guilty look at the Dry Rite Cleaners over there on the left. In spite of their amateur efforts to improve the outside, the place still looked kind of run-down. He himself had washed and polished the large front windows until they glittered. Even ol' Phoebe had come over two Saturdays ago and dug up the neglected bushes in front of the shop, put in new dirt and planted a little bunch of crispy hedges. Definitely made the outside look better. The inside had also been double-scrubbed, ready for new paint as soon as they could afford it.

But the trouble was, he knew from hearing the folks talk that the shop needed a ton of other stuff, too: better lighting, up-to-date electrical hookups, and most importantly new, expensive machines.

The lean, sober-faced man at the bank had said that he needed to see if the business would pick up before he could loan them "a sizable amount" of money. He made it apparent that he didn't want to back a loser, and he also let them know that most of the townspeople were still taking their clothes over to Milltown, nine miles away—so how could they pay him back?

A-K tightened his grip on the handlebars. Well, of course he'd help more if his parents asked him to. But no way was he going to volunteer. Not after his dad—typical, typical – had told him last week that his attempts to help around the place were slipshod.

Nope, the folks'd better hire professionals. People who got

paid to be insulted.

When he arrived at the gliderport, it seemed like the only action going was out there in the field. The same spotted cows were still lumbering around. Realizing how early it was, he was tempted to walk over and strike up a conversation with them, just to pass the time.

Do cows like people? Kinna nice faces and they seem friendly, too, so maybe–hey, no, he told himself! Don't go out there, you'll look like a jerk, if anybody catches you.

Bright sunlight was beginning to stream down from the tree tops onto the still-wet grass. A single power plane, parked out-aways, winked and flashed in the buttery light. And up here–alright! Three long trailers had arrived since last Tuesday, each as long as two beds together, with peaked roofs at the end of each of them. Had to be, for the vertical tail fins.

Best thing was seeing a yellow glider parked up close here, at the beginning of the grass runway. It wasn't there last time. Maybe the one he'd be flying? Man, it sure was a beaut!

After his walk-around, A-K parked himself on the bottom step of the office trailer and flipped through Grogan's glider manual again. He'd read it clear through three times already, almost had it memorized.

"Mornin' Andor!" Mr. Grogan called, getting out of his aging car a half an hour later. "So how's with you?"

"Real fine, sir. Looks like a great day to fly, right?" Wished he had the nerve to ask the instructor not to call him Andor. Maybe later.

"Yep, sure looks like it. Well, let's get inside and warm up. These Fall mornings, you know..." Grogan collected up a stack of folders from the station wagon's front seat. No comments about his student's being out here so early. Following him, A-K smiled. It was starting!

Inside the office, the burly manager fired up a little oil heater, then handed A-K a narrow, fake-leather booklet.

"Sit down over there, son." Waving at one of the bus seats, Grogan said firmly, "Now look: this is going to be your own personal logbook. You'll keep track of exactly where you flew, how long it took–weather conditions, any problems. Gotta write it all down. A permanent record, required by the FAA–that's the Federal Aviation Administration."

A permanent record? Geez, what if he screwed up? Would that be written down, too?

After filling out the required page, A-K ventured, "I, um, guess I got here kinna early, sir. So maybe I'll explore around a li'l bit, if that's okay..." With the papers in front of him, Grogan nodded and A-K took himself outside again.

Soon after, an SUV rumbled into the parking lot. This sharp looking guy got out – looked like he could be some actor on TV, with his tight jeans, leather jacket and cowboy hat. Nodding to A-K, he hustled up the steps and pretty soon there were bursts of laughter coming from inside the trailer.

By ten o'clock, a little crowd had lined themselves up behind the wire-mesh fence: One kid, three grownups, and a Dalmatian dog –the kind of people he'd often stood around with at the small airport in Tucson. The Watchers.

Something fizzed up inside him. But not me, not today!

"All right, Andor. Now, let's get down to business." Walking toward the plane with him half an hour later the burly instructor told him, "Your glider lesson's gonna be in that two-seater out there. It's called a Schweizer. The crew calls it the yellow banana. We'll start with the preflight. You read all that material I sent home?"

"Yes sir." By now, he'd read the brief training booklet several times over. "Preflight's checkin' out all the moving parts and..." (Slow down, Kerzak, he told himself, quit tryin' to show-off) "... and also the control surfaces, making sure nothing's stuck or broken, 'fore the take-off."

"Good! You've been studying. Okay, here comes the lecture," Grogan said, standing by the plane. "I give it to everybody, the first time. 'Course, you're not expected to remember this stuff all'n one day. But pay attention."

"In gliders, and sailplanes too, it's the ailerons, the stick and the rudders, that do the flying. In the air, they operate the parts of the wing and the tail that let you go up or down, or turn right or left."

The instructor shrugged. "She's not exactly what you'd call sleek, like some of these fiberglass ships they're making nowdays, but you can count on her. This bird is real steady."

Rubbing his large sunburned nose, Mr. Grogan talked about thermals and sunshine. "Columns of warm rising air from the ground are what keep a glider up," he said. "A lot of talk 'round here about up-drafts and lift, heated air. You catch some under your ship and you rise up. Pretty nice, huh?"

A long-ish pause. "Then, of course," Grogan added, "there're also downdrafts, right?"

A-K nodded solemnly. Taking a deep breath, he pictured the crash of his beautiful, broken Condor again. Smashed to pieces. What his plane had needed that day was a better pilot.

Soon, he was helping Grogan drag the large glider out to the grassy runway on its single wheel. Together, they gently rolled it over onto its right side again and Grogan resumed the lesson.

Walking around the ship with his clipboard, the instructor spent over forty minutes, carefully explaining which inside controls worked which outside parts of the two wings and the tail.

Finally, A-K was told to climb in the slanted front seat and strap himself inside the still-open cockpit. He'd been worried his legs might not be quite long enough to reach the rudder pedals, but it turned out the seat was adjustable and it slid forward just fine.

Leaning against the outside door, Grogan named the three main instruments on the front panel - the airspeed indicator – altimeter and the veriometer, and described what they did.

Even though his heart was beating so hard he was afraid the instructor could hear it, A-K concentrated on what Grogan was saying. The boy kept repeating, "right-right" and "yes sir, I see " at what he was being told.

The older man exchanged a few serious words with the tow

pilot who was standing by – turned out it was that swanky dude with the cowboy hat–and then the instructor huffed himself into the back seat of the glider.

Climbing into the front seat, A-K stared at the dials up in front of him. Whew, he thought, this stuff's complicated. Still, Tina's brother wasn't older than me when he started. Guess I can try it.

Next, the tow pilot strode past them and swung himself up into the red-winged Super Cub. Soon, with a steady growl, the power plane taxied past the yellow glider, moving directly in front of them. Then, as if out of nowhere, this frizzy-haired kid just appeared and connected a long tow rope between the two planes.

Then the tall kid walked around to the left side of them and stood there blank-faced, like an acolyte waiting for the priest.

C'mon, A-K thought irritably, the jerk's gotta get out of the way . What's he hangin' around for?

Twisting sideways, he saw the instructor roll the rounded plexiglass canopy over them, nice and snug, then snap it in place. Next, Grogan gave a thumbs-up to the fellow outside. Calmly, the helper outside grabbed the low wing and pulled it up until the two wings were level.

Oh, yeah, now I get it, A-K told himself. He's part of the deal.

"See," Grogan called from the back. "Lifting the down wing up, gets us level, and also tells the pilot up ahead we're ready to go. You watch: our friend out there's gonna run alongside us 'til we lift off the ground."

With his free hand, the kid outside motioned in wide, slow circles to the pilot up in front. In position, the two connected planes began their roll down the runway. Holding onto the one wing, the line boy raced right along with them.

CHAPTER 6

Gaining more speed, the towplane roared down the runway. The guy who'd been running alongside the glider suddenly released the Schweizer's wing tip and dropped back.

Then, with no warning, the glider leaped a few feet above the grass, briefly higher than the still earth-bound power plane. A-K's tense face suddenly relaxed as he felt the slide from the land to the sky.

"Hey I'm doin' it, man." he whispered to himself. He felt like he'd been waiting for this moment all his life.

Up ahead, the Super Cub took charge, as if : enough of this, you upstart glider. Now, I'm running the show. The single-engine plane slid up into the morning sky, pulling the yellow glider behind it with its two hundred-foot long rope.

On the panel in front of A-K, the needles circled around the dials, slow and steady as the glider headed up and up. Fifteen hundred, then two thousand feet, the wind tore past the canopy with a high, singing sound.

"Gods, feels like we're headin' for the top of the world," A-K whispered. Then he hunched up his shoulders, telling himself: Oh sure.

"Three thousand feet, Ronvold. That's it!" Grogan called into his hand-held radio. "Thanks, ol' buddy."

"O-*kaa-y* , Andor," the instructor said loudly, "pull out the red knob I showed you. Time for us to let loose."

There was a clanking, metal *bang* sound on release. The Super Cub wig-wagging goodbye with its shiny red wings, banked and dove away to the left. The pale rope whipped behind the tow plane like a kite tail.

With an unsteady breath, A-K studied the panel in front of him. The altimeter read "3", exactly. Yeah, that made sense. Every time the needle came around full circle, they'd climbed up another thousand feet from the ground. It was all in that book Grogan had loaned him.

"Pretty great, huh?" Grogan called up as he worked the control stick from the back. All the instructor's moves, duplicated in front, even with no hands on, were slow and gentle. First, going to the right, he made a slow, smooth turn. Then a turn to the left. Up front, A-K's control column moved right along with the back one.

He wondered if all two-man gliders worked like this or if this one was special, just for teaching.

Not the time to ponder though, because, except for the whoosh-sound, outside, a sudden quiet had settled down on them. Now it felt as if they were floating on still water. "This's just... so totally cool," the boy offered through his microphone. He wished he could tell it better but didn't know how.

Edging over to the right side of the plane, more relaxed, he peered down. The houses and cars down there looked like some kid had just left his junk all over the place.

Seconds later, passing the town, he saw a glittering web of ditches running through the dry September fields. Off to the east, comforting hay-colored hills, then the darker mountains, stretched up and away.

And, except for a soft whoosh of wind, the sound of a boomerang hurled through space, it was peaceful and quiet outside the canopy.

Too dang quiet. A-K thought, bolting up. Hey, there's no motor in this thing. If we fall down outta here, we'll... we'll die! Shrinking inside his webbed harness, he tried to get hold of himself. Lookit, Kerzak, he told himself, ya just read about this stuff. Gliders float on an "ocean of air." Said so, right in that book last night. We're okay.

"All right, Andor," Grogan boomed from the back, "Let's do us some flyin' now. I want you to put one hand lightly on the stick, then, both feet on the rudders, but don't push 'em. Remember, we have the same controls. To start with, I'll still be working the controls from the back."

Now they turned and flew west, with the glider's nose just below the horizon. The wind had increased and the choppy water of Lake Washington was dotted with billowing white sails. Beyond was the long, narrow city, then the enclosed, gray-blue ocean of Puget Sound.

From this distance, Seattle looked like a toy-town built out of kindergarten blocks. It was mostly tall and small columns tipped with triangular roofs, glass-faced towers, circular hotels and that goofy Space Needle. Water on both sides made it look as if it were a floating city.

Gradually, A-K became aware that the stick in front of him was being regularly moved by the instructor's hand behind him. Back and forth, up and sideways, it moved in a sort of slow circle. Under his feet, the rudder pedals moved, too. It reminded him of Dad, who kept the car's steering wheel constantly in play while making endless adjustments with his feet.

"Okay, son," Grogan called up. "Want you to tell me what happens when I–gent-ly–pull back on the stick."

"Well, the uh, the nose lifts up?"

"Correct. And notice, we also slow down some. Feel it?"

"Yes, sir. Sure do." He swallowed, hoping Grogan wouldn't pull the stick back any further. Might drop 'em out of the sky.

"Good. And when I push the stick forward a little –noth-ing sud-den–what happens?"

"We go–downhill?"

"Exactly. And also we go faster. Now, let's try turning left, then right, at the same levels." The instructor paused, then thunked a light fist on the rigid back in front of him. "Relax, son. This is s'posed to be fun!"

Forcing a laugh, A-K unbunched his shoulders. He inched the stick to the left.

"That's it," from the back. "So, to go left, to bank left is how we say it, ya slowly push the stick, left, and at the same time, now, push the left rudder down with your foot. Not much, not much - that's it! Jus' take your time."

With his left foot pressed on the floor rudder, and with a "light touch on the stick" as he'd read in the book, A-K saw the left yellow wing slant downwards and green fir and cedar-studded hills angle into view. Then, when told to lift his foot, they leveled off again, smooth as silk. Ni-ice.

"To go right," Grogan continued from the back seat, "we do the opposite. Push the stick over to the right, add a little right rudder–slowly-does-it-gently."

Off to the south, the snowy Mt. Rainier rose up like a gigantic scoop of ice cream; gradually it spread out, then patted itself down into lowlands.

"Okay, Andor, I want you to take over for a while. You be the pilot. Up for it ?"

A-K's mouth instantly went dry and he had a sudden urge to pee. Still, this lesson was costing him big bucks.

"I–I guess so, sir," he croaked.

"Right! So, now–do nothing fast. You want to keep us straight-and-level." Using the floor rudders, Grogan had him practice more turns. "Bank in one direction, then turn, go the other way. See! Gradually, it pushes the nose down, slowly takes her up."

The tightness in A-K's neck let go a little. Hey, this isn't so hard, he thought, straightening up. Geez Louise, Mr. Grogan's actually let me fly!

They were on a smooth down-hill glide now. The easy sound of wind made him feel almost sleepy. Things were going fantastic.

"Hey! We're going too slow,"the instructor shouted suddenly. "Drop the nose, son, drop it NOW, gotta get up the airspeed. Only doing forty. At thirty–we can stall out!"

Stall out? Oh gods, he'd read about that. Kiss of death. Breakin' air flow. Crashing.

A-K squeezed the stick until the veins popped out in his hand. Trouble was, he'd forgotten if he was supposed to push it forward or pull it backwards. *He couldn't remember how to drop the nose.*

"Don't worry," Grogan yelled up. "I've got it."

It was a blur after that. As the stick was pushed forward, the glider swooped like a porpoise taking a dive. Sweat beaded A-K's upper lip and he could feel his shirt sticking to his back. The rudder pedals were being worked under his feet without his help; outside, the wind's scary, high-pitched sounds.

Seconds later, the plane leveled out again. The shrill wind grew quieter. The airspeed indicator moved up to a safe fifty-five miles an hour.

"See, you've got to think, now. With the nose up"–the instructor's voice was firm but he didn't sound mad or anything–"your air speed goes down, because it's working against the wind. With the nose down, air speed goes up. Say it to yourself a few times. Nose down, speed's up, nose up, speed's down. Mostly it's good old gravity, like riding a bike up and down hills."

In the middle of Grogan's sentence, the Schweizer took another funny lurch, a sharp jolt as if they'd just run over one of those man-made speed bumps on a roadway. A-K swiveled his head, wanting to read Grogan's expression, but he couldn't turn his body around far enough. Instead, he started muttering Hail Marys.

"All right! " Grogan shouted in a happy voice. "We've caught us a big fat thermal. Hang on to your socks, son–we're headin' up."

Lifted by a vaulting current of air, the Schweizer spiraled higher and higher in wide, lazy circles. The variometer kept going around, up, up, slow and steady. As they climbed, A-K, narrow-eyed, just couldn't stop smiling.

WOW, he thought, no big ol' show-off power plane out there, pullin' us up, now. Just the natural world. Feels like I'm some kind of a - *ghost pilot.*

Letting his mind wander, A-K smiled. Yeah, like ol' Casper the Ghost. Not a bad life except, guess he was kinna dead. No, then he came back.

Continuing the wide turns, rising steadily through all of them, Grogan called from the back seat, "Getta look at the altimeter, will ya! We got ourselves another thousand feet. It's a thermal, comin' up from those fields down there. Remember, in a glider, heat and wind'll push ya up."

Breathing through his mouth, feeling happier than he could ever remember, A-K nodded. "Man oh man," he whispered, "I wouldn't mind stayin' up here all day!"

"Well, hate to say it," the instructor announced, all too soon, "but we've got to go back now. Been up here over forty minutes. Wouldn't you know, just when the lift gets really going? But I've got another lesson comin' up pretty quick. Maybe another time."

As Grogan eased the stick forward, A-K checked out the side window again. Okay, now remember, he told himself: those things stickin' out from the wings–it's not ailerons, they're dive brakes. Gotta another funny name, too. Oh yeah - spoilers. That training book said they work like a reverse engine to slow us down more.

Sweeping high over the golden hills, first they flew away from the field, on downwind, and then the instructor flew them on base, lining up with the field. "On this last turn," the instructor called up, "we're heading straight into the wind, on 'final'."

They touched down, gently. The two of them slid across the grass on the plane's single wheel: rightrudder leftrudder, right left ri-ii-ght le-ft and–STOP ! Lacking two wheels to balance it, the yellow glider gently tipped over on the right wing again.

The opened canopy let in a flood of warm sweet air. It smelled of hot grasses and plowed fields. Breathing deeply, tired, A-K sat there a while longer, inhaling the tangy whiffs of what smelled like burning cedar chips. Must be from those lumber mills up the road. Oh man, he thought–maybe living here isn't going to be all that bad.

Grogan huffed his bulky self out of the rear seat. Instead of hurrying away, though, the red-headed man came up and rested a plump hand on the slanted fuselage a minute. "You did fine, son. Made some nice banks, and, mostly, kep' your cool."

"Yeah, well, I dunno," A-K mumbled. "Sure flubbed up on the stick that time."

"So? Concentrate on what you did right. Look here, Andor–

you can't learn magic by watching a magician. First you've got to try things, make the mistakes. Then you'll know what to look for. That's what Orville Wright said, and he was the guy who knew!"

It crossed A-K's mind to blurt out that he would never forget the instructor, that this ride had been the best thing he'd done in his entire life, that he'd never felt as happy as he was today, up in the sky. But of course, he didn't. Kerzaks didn't act like that, running around telling how they felt about stuff.

"It was good, it was really good, sir," the boy managed. "Thank you."

Concerned about the next lesson he had to teach, Grogan hurried back to the office-trailer, but A-K didn't go anywhere. Not right away. He felt as if his bones had just up and left his body. Besides the tiredness, he could feel a strong pulse throbbing on the side of his neck.

He could do better next time, he knew he could. Study up on those books. Figure out which parts of the glider did what. Get it all memorized. And then, even getting scared wouldn't foul him up.

"See—all I want is just the one lesson," A-K had assured his folks. Mainly, he'd told the same thing to Grogan. "Kinna curious about what it's like, you know..." And he'd definitely meant it too, at the time.

But now, after taking just this one single trip, A-K resolved that even if nothin' else in this entire universe worked out, he was gonna learn to fly. And not just when he was an old guy: Now!

CHAPTER 7

"Hey, Space Ace, lemme have the ballast outta there, will you? Boss says we don't need it for the next lesson."

Still buckled up in the front seat, A-K was surprised the line boy had gotten up so close without his noticing. Man, he thought, looking at him up so close – you could scrub out a frying pan with the top of this guy's head.

His hair reminded A-K of the curls his mother made out of paper ribbon, scraping it with a sharp knife. If this had been a friend back home, he'd of had a lot of fun kidding the big string bean.

But not out here, not when you're new. Might get busted in the nose.

"Sure, I'll get it," A-K said. "So – where is it exactly?" Mr. Grogan hadn't mentioned a ballast.

"Down there, by the rudder pedals. Your feet are prac'ly on top of it." The tall boy didn't look very friendly.

A-K, who'd never been in any kind of harness before, tried to shake himself out of the rig he was in. Then, frustrated, he attempted to yank it off but the straps were too tight. Sweating now, embarrassed, he lurched forward planning to grab up the solid pillow-looking thing and maybe lift it up with his feet.

Trouble was, A-K couldn't reach down that far.

"Lemme show you a trick," the kid said. He leaned into the cockpit and yanked open the metal latch below A-K's ribs. "Now let's see what'cha can do."

"Right!" A-K muttered, still tangled up in the top and bottom layers of straps. Was he supposed to connect them up behind him now, or just let 'em lay?

"Hey, no insult," the line boy said, "but looks like you're fightin' an octopus, man, and you're losing.

Swearing, refusing to even look at the know-it-all, A-K finally figured his way out of the straps. Then, confidently, he grabbed up the gray weight and attempted to stand right up with it. Somehow though, probably because of the narrowness of the cockpit, he lost his balance and collapsed back into the seat.

The line boy reached for the ballast but A-K waved him off. Climbing out, almost falling, with the gray ballast still in his hands, he managed to land on his feet. In the process, though, he dropped the weight on the grass.

"Yeah! Well, sure hope this wasn't some kinna I.Q. test," A-K said, trying to regain his dignity. Bending over he picked up the ballast-weight and dusted it off on his clean shirt. "Because if it was, I just bombed Gettin Outta Big Yellow Glider 101."

The line boy studied him a second. Then, straight-faced, he said, "Well, now that you mention it, yeah, it was a major test. But lookit, ya gimme a wad of money, I keep my mouth shut about you bein' a flunk-out."

A-K could handle this stuff; it was like talking to his buddies back home. "Zat right?" he retorted. "Well, that's no surprise. Even in Arizona where I used to live, I heard all about the graft and corruption you got out here."

Now he was having to speed-walk to keep up with the guy's long stride, but it was fun.

"I was jus' kiddin', ya know about the graft part." the line boy told him. "But it is right, about the income. I don't make a dime out here. Grogan can't afford to pay anybody but the tow pilot." He sighed. "So, new subject: you picked up some good thermals t'day. How'd ya like it?"

Quickly A-K thought back to the book he borrowed. Thermals - like when the sun heats up in a plowed field or a bunch of rocks, the air shoots up, he remembered. You get above that kind of stuff in a light plane, it pushes you up with it. Yeah: *hot air rises*

"It was okay," he mumbled as they crossed the field together. Then he stole another look at the guy and decided to take a chance. "Heard them calling you 'Heck' this morning. Someone cussing you out or is that your name?"

"Probably both," the curly-haired fellow replied. "It's Heck as in 'heck of a sexy guy'. An' you got a name?"

"Yeah. Officially, it's Andor Kerzak But A-K works better. And no Polak jokes. I've heard 'em all. Folks are Hungarian."

Without missing a beat, Heck drawled, "Got it. Okay, so here's an airport joke for ya: What's the diff'rence 'tween a boat and a glider?"

Water and air both make 'em sail away? No, he'd said what's the difference. A-K slowed down, trying to pull out a killer answer.

"Well," he said, catching back up, "how about – one floats on the water, other one floats in the air?" Not totally funny but he thought it was pretty good.

"Wrong wrong wrong," the kid cried. "Ya don't win the jack-pot. Ya don't collect the forty thousan' dollars. Sor-ry."

"Oh, yeah? Then let's hear the big answer." A-K wondered if the guy went to the same school he did. Looked about the right age. And he wouldn't come clear out here from Milltown, would he? Be way too far, by bike. Naw, he probably lives in St. Clair, same as me. Wonder if he knows that Tina?

"The answer IS – " Heck announced, "one lands on the ground, one grounds on the land "

A-K did some fast thinking. "Pitiful!" he announced. "That joke's a total hamburger!" After a brief pause, he added, "Ground round, hamburger, don' cha get it?" Almost like talking to his friends back in Tucson.

"Interesting," Heck said in a flat voice "Now tell me a funny one."

Feeling easier, A-K said, "Nuther time. So - how long've you been working here, anyway?"

"Since the end of April, when the other guy moved away."

The other guy? Sounded like they only needed one line boy at a time. Bummer.

Using the ballast as an excuse, he followed Heck up to the wide door of a small metal shed. Blinking, he peered into the warm shadows while Heck heaved the plastic weight onto a pile

of others. What were they for, anyway? Keep the glider from going up too high? Well, don't ask, A-K told himself; no need to
advertise all the stuff you don't know.

"Bet it's kinna cool having a job like yours," he volunteered
from the shed's door.

"Oh sure." said Heck.

Then he dragged an empty oil barrel away from the door,
rolling it into a corner. Suddenly he threw the whole batch of oily
towels at the newcomer. Surprised, A-K managed to catch all but
one.

"Good reflexes! Why don'cha fold these up for me, since
you're hangin' around anyway. It's one of the real cool jobs us
line boys get ta do."

Shrugging, A-K walked all the way into the shed. He sat down
under a slice of sun coming through a hole in the metal roof above
them., and folded the small towels, smelling of fuel oil, first in
thirds, then into messy origami packages.

"Actually, yeah, it's a decent job." Watching the new kid create the grubby fold-ups, Heck added, "Not that we make any
money, don' get me wrong. Like I said, the boss barely makes
expenses as it is. This is loggin' country and around here, the
buildin' trade's way off."

Right. A-K knew, from the talk around his own dinner table,
that St. Clair wasn't famous for being a rich place. Already Dad
was worried that even if he got some regular customers, a lot of
them wouldn't be able pay their bills.

"But what Grogan does is pay us back'n air time," Heck added,
running a hand over his bushy hair.

"Air time? You mean you get free lessons ?" A-K started re-
folding his pile of towels one more time so Heck wouldn't send
him away. Least, not until he heard the answer.

"Yep, well, every once in a while." The guy sounded a little
smug.

"Huh! Well, do you think Mr. Grogan ever wants, I mean,
needs – you know, could use extra help? Like in the summer or
something?"

"No way, Jose," Heck said quickly. "We're all full up."

While the line boy was delivering this news, A-K suddenly heard the rumble of the power plane close outside. Sounded like another tow going up.

A-K scrambled up from the dirt floor, anxious to see the take-off. "How come you're not out there?" he asked over his shoulder. "Thought you were this big-deal line boy."

"Because that plane's comin' in , not goin' out," Heck said calmly. He shoved all the folded towels into a falling-apart wicker basket. "Can'cha even hear the difference?"

CHAPTER 8

Standing in the noisy cafeteria line with no one to talk to, A-K felt more lonely than ever. But who cares, he told himself. Pushing each other out of line, their stupid jokes, I don't need 'em.

Stone-faced, he suddenly noticed a particular small girl up there, just three people ahead. It was definitely that Tina Beckman! Somebody to talk to – if she remembered him.

Reaching over the counter, he snatched up one of the prepared lunch trays and made plans to travel. Yeah, he could tell her about going out to the field she'd told him about. Maybe impress her, him being a man of action.

So all he had to do was keep working his way past the dodos in front of him and play it cool, like: Oh, hi. Tina! Haven't seen you since my lesson and oh yeah, I went ahead and...

Oops! Hey, what's happening?

One of the guys up ahead, maybe to punctuate a story he was telling his friend, suddenly threw back his left arm. The motion knocked A-K's tray straight out of his hands. All the food hit the floor. The salad and the hard roll took off sideways; the wax carton lay on its side, bleeding milk. Most of the hot chili piled up on the gray linoleum like orange mud. The near-empty pottery bowl didn't break; it just kind of rocked around gently, no fuss.

The fuss came from the arm-swinger. "Hey, shrimp," the guy yelled in this outraged voice. "What'er you tryin' to do, anyway? Cuttin' in? Tell ya right now, that crap on the floor idn't my fault!"

"Yeah, shrimp!" the friend chimed in loyally.

Of course, because of the way A-K's luck was going, that Tina (oh man, it was her), glanced back to see what the ruckus was about. And not just her: seemed like half the people in the whole cafeteria were looking at him. When the long-haired girl spotted him down on his hands and knees trying to scrape up the orange smelly mess with his one napkin, she shook her head sympathetically, although she also looked as if she thought it was a little funny, too.

Anyway, no time to worry: the next "fun" action came from these four or five guys down the line who started bombarding him with paper napkin airplanes. A regular blizzard. Napkins weren't much help though. What A-K needed were rags and a bucket of soapy water, which he finally got from the kitchen, along with a commercial-sized mop.

Red-faced, he mopped backwards away from the long tables, hoping maybe the kids wouldn't remember who'd made all this mess.

The whole deal, far as he was concerned, was about as private as having a circus march through town. All that was missing were the elephants.

And he was the clown.

When he'd finally cleaned every last speck of it up, A-K went back to the kitchen door and got a new tray. Terrific. He was so late now, it looked like there wasn't one seat left.

"Hey, Andor," a vaguely-familiar voice called from one of the back tables. "A seat, back here."

Now, who...oh yeah! It was that kid with the crazy hair, the gliderport guy. What was his name? Some kinna swear word. Next to him was a nerdy-lookin' kid with coke-bottle glasses, scarfing up his lunch. Nevermind – a rescue.

Relieved, A-K carried his second lunch of the day across the large, breathy room and plopped down next to the two boys.

"I see you didn't like what they were servin' today, right?" the gliderport fellow commented.

A-K gobbled down several spoonfuls of the luke-warm chili, then waving his spoon in the air he informed them, "Nuh-uh, that's not it. I'll do anything for attention."

That shut them up for a minute. Then the mophead boy remarked, "Well, that's great, 'cause you're gonna be gettin' more of it. Attention, I mean. Hear the Principal wants to see ya, right after lunch. Got your parents in his office ri'now."

Heck, that was his name. Half-believing him, A-K looked over but what he saw in the guy's big-boned face was: Got'cha! A-K flattened his lips together and nodded.

Obviously pleased with himself, Heck introduced him to his friend, Boz Davis. "So meet the new kid, Andor Something."

Boz murmured, "Hey."

"Hi," A-K said in a tired voice. "By the way, Andor is just official, you know, like when the police need to pick me up or something. Mainly, I'm called A-K, all right?"

Shrugging, Boz nodded, then looked away. A shy guy.

Meanwhile, Heck began to try and rub a blob of chili off his new-looking shirt. He was cussing quietly to himself as he did it. When he gave up, the orange color was not coming out, even with spit, He looked up and said in a flat voice, "Just your initials, huh? O-kay, A-K, you got it."

"And actually, that little routine with the chili?" A-K said, cheering up again. "See, it usually goes better with *jello*. But, damn they just weren't serving any today."

"Ya don' say!" Now Heck's face lit up with approval like, least the new guy knows how to handle himself. Boz nodded, too.

The two friends went back to a conversation they'd started earlier. Boz was trying to locate a cheap radiator for the junker he and his brother were repairing. Immediately, Heck proposed a trip out to the town dump, said there were plenty of old cars out there they could cannibalize for just a few bucks.

As A-K wolfed down the remains of his salad, he wondered if these guys might invite him to come along sometime. One of his favorite places in Tucson was the dump.

"Hey, McCallister," someone called across the room as the bulky football player came strutting in. Marko was surrounded, as usual, by some of his big-deal friends: Lowinsen, Sackett and Joe Wilder. Upper classmen, big deal, all of them. Even A-K knew who they were by now.

Smooth-looking, self-assured, these were the guys who

seemed to run the school. Everybody talked about them, tried to copy their clothes and the way they talked. Cluing the new kid in, Heck told him that Marko sometimes got to play first-string on the school's football team (as did Dirk Lowinsen). He mentioned that McCallister was older than most of the Juniors because of his year's-long trip to Europe one time.

On a roll, Heck went on to tell him old man McCallister who had the Cadillac-Chrysler business out there on the highway, also owned the "coolest plane around." He kept it out at the little airport, across from Grogan's field.

"He's got a sailplane?'

"Naw, I said at the far end. Where the power planes are. Gots one of those speedy, low-wing jobs, a red Mooney, four-seater. Retractable gear. She's a real beaut, I'm tellin' ya." Heck ran his finger along his plate, scraping up the last of the chili sauce and popped it into his mouth.

"Sometimes," he went on, wiping his hand on his jeans, "his dad flies him and maybe a buddy up to the San Juan Islands or Canada, places like that. Jus' to go fishing!"

Imagine having your own plane, A-K thought. Wonder if Mr. McCallister's teaching Marko to fly? Probably. For the first time since he'd laid eyes on that loud mouth, he felt the stirrings of envy.

Across the cafeteria, Tina and her chattering girl friends got ready to leave. Made him think of a flock of birds. A-K gazed at her a moment, then looked away. Forget it, Kerzak, he told himself. After this chili stunt, she's gotta think you're a jerk, if she didn't before.

Marko, who hadn't bothered to line up with his class yet, was still busy hogging center stage. He strutted over to the group of girls. A-K saw the bulky football player start kidding Tina about something or other. He even got her to laugh.

Well, it figured: the top guys always got the best girls. Suppressing a sigh, he got up and followed Heck and Boz, who were finishing up a batch of light bulb jokes. Real squares, both of them, but they were nice. Seemed decent, maybe friend material.

At dinner that night, Viktor Kerzak kept pushing his food around with his fork, not eating. His face was pinched white around his mouth. Mom had put out a really good dinner, too – a spicy stew, salad and home-made rolls, which usually made a hit with the family – but the vibes felt funny tonight. A-K started checking back, wondering if he'd screwed up lately. Couldn't think of anything special, but it was usually him Dad was mad at.

Rubbing one of his Keds up against the other, he thought about calling up that lady psychologist on the radio to see if she had any ideas about how to improve 'family relations'. Would she talk to a teenager? Well, just to be on the safe side, he wouldn't tell her how old he was.

"Zose Milton Cleaners!" his father burst out. He clanged his fork down. "You know vot they've done now?"

"No dear, what?" Mom asked in her soft voice.

"They bought themselfs a delivery truck, that's vot! On Saturday, but I'm just finding out today. You know vy they did it?"

"Well, I can guess. They're probably going to start pick-up and delivery. Maybe we should do that too, when we can afford it. What do you think? Why, if..."

With an edge of hysteria in his voice, Dad interrupted, "No, not jus' for Milltown. It's so zey can come into our town. Coming ofer *here*, to Saint Clair, to steal our customers!"

Heating up, he added, "Ja! – they're like thoze soldiers, banging themselfs into my..."

"Shhhh, shhh shhush ," said his mother. "Victor! Don't be ridiculous. It's not the same." She dodged A-K's eyes, staying focused on her husband. Her intense look said: stop this talk.

A-K had heard bits and pieces of the 'bad old days' – but where? Maybe from his parents talking with the Zaleys back in Tucson. Probably more of the war stuff. Come on, he thought, sliding the rest of his beets under a lettuce leaf. Get a life, Dad. The Russians were a real long time ago. You've gotta let go of that stuff.

A-K shifted in his chair. But that idea of delivering the clothes, well, he'd thought of it too. A great idea! He'd even gone so far as to call the DMV when they'd first moved out here. Over the phone, they'd said he could drive a truck when he was sixteen-and-a-half, and when he had a commercial license.

Yeah, he could fix up their V. W. bus with racks clear up to the ceiling, yank out the back seats and make room for the long stuff. He could blast around town, delivering. It would probably be fun, but it'd be helping too. The jobs he did now – windows once in a while, carting out the trash different times, wiping the counters down with Hexol – were still way more than he'd done back in Arizona.

Now, sliding down in his chair, he submerged himself in one of his favorite daydreams. He was in this huge air show, flying in a Mooney heading straight up at the sun! Then, while crowds below were holding their breath and closing their eyes, *he* starts making loop-the-loops way above them. Aiming straight for the ground like a Kamikaze pilot, he'd turn away at the last minute. People were so scared they were screaming...

No, here's what it is, A-K revised: Tina would be there, maybe with her mother. She'd say: *"Why, I never knew A-K could fly like that! But Mom, see, he's the kind of person who doesn't go around bragging every minute. Quiet, you know, but he does the most amazing stuff..."*

Through all the imaginary haze of aerial smoke, A-K heard his mother announce, "Viktor, you have to fight them!"

A-K blinked and sat straight up. Had he heard right? Annyuka, little mother, trying to give advice – to Dad?

It surprised his father, too. "Fight them?" The gray-haired man glared at her with incredulous eyes. "An' jus' how do you suggest I do zat, Missus Know-Everysing?"

His mother hesitated, then she plunged in: "Join things, that's how. Meet people. Show them we want to be good neighbors. The Lions Club invited you, you said no. The Toastmasters invited you, you said no to them, too."

"Right, Dad," A-K chimed in. "You gotta advertise."

"Vell, it's too late now," his father told them both. He sat back in his chair, crossing his thin legs. "I vas ast, already. Nobody asts you two times."

"Well, nevermind," Mom went on, doggedly. "Father Tom, at the church? He told me there's a men's breakfast group, meets early on Thursday mornings. Why don't you join, Viktor? Make some friends. It'll also remind the town that the cleaners has been re-opened."

Later, up in his small bedroom, what A-K remembered best was the part where his mother told Dad: Stop grousin' around, and do something!

Downstairs, the sad Hungarian music his father listened to almost every night drifted upstairs. It was as familiar a sound as hearing the daily news on TV, or, now that they lived here, as familiar as the daily blasts from the cedar mill. Drowsily, A-K wondered if his father might ever, in this life (or even in the next one) get up the nerve to try anything risky.

CHAPTER 9

Friday night, A-K had watched television way past midnight, so this morning he felt like being lazy. Stretched out like a zombie, he watched the early sunlight bob around on the ceiling. He felt kind of like being under water. It was quiet downstairs. Saturday. Folks must be at work.

But for him, it was a free day. Last night he'd worked nearly three hours, putting away a bunch of supplies at the shop. Yeah, he thought, bet most of the kids around here don't help their families even half as much as I do.

Finally, when he did get himself out of bed, he wandered over to the window. Oh man, he thought, just look at that sky! What'd it say in that flying book? Popper... no. Those're *popcorn* clouds out there – which means lift. He remembered from reading in one of those books he'd borrowed that rising heat makes those kinds of clouds. Thermals. Turned loose from tow, a glider had a chance of climbing up in the sky maybe thousands of feet. Fast, rising air could send you up like a feather over a heat vent.

On a day like this, he was pretty sure some of those hotshot pilots Heck kept talkin' about would show up.

After putting on some mismatched clothes, A-K gobbled a bowl of Cheerios down in the kitchen, stuffed a handful of dried apricots in one of his jacket pockets and, hopping on his bike, headed straight for the gliderport. He wondered if he'd have skipped school if today were a Tuesday or something. Maybe...

A-K looked around: the ride out here was sure worth it. Lots of people out here today. The dirt parking lot was nearly full-up. Besides Grogan's old Mustang, there were six other cars, a light-blue pickup truck, an empty horse trailer and a couple of tail-wagging dogs. Yeah, so maybe the crew might need some extra help.

Out there on the field Grogan and a grown man not much bigger than A-K were busy walking around the Schweizer. From the parking lot, the boy ardently watched, as the instructor pointed to different parts of the trainer plane.

Twenty minutes later, with Grogan and the student almost ready to go, ol' Heck marched out onto the grass runway and attached the Super Cub's long tow rope onto the glider's nose. Ron had the power plane rumbling up ahead by now, and was waiting to move forward. The line boy, noticing the new kid was here again, got a funny look on his face. But after a minute, he nodded anyway. Watching the procedure some more, A-K told himself: I could do that, job's not all that hard.

Heck didn't own the place.

A lot of action out here! People kept driving in like it was bargain day at the Seattle Mall. Down near one of the metal sheds, he spotted a tall pilot just starting to put his glider together. Big, friendly face, no hair on his head. None.

The man's white two-seater fuselage had been dragged off its trailer though the canopy was still closed. Trying to look inconspicuous, A-K meandered over and watched quietly for several minutes. Then, getting up his nerve, he asked quietly, "Sir? Can I – could you use an extra hand?" No need to mention he wasn't part of the crew.

"Right on! Yeah! Can't say no to that!" The grown-up grinned, flashing a row of large, white teeth. Way he talked, the man didn't seem all that old.

"Hey, nice of you to offer. My name's Doc Kingsbury, but some folks call me Baldy Locks. And who are you, please?"

"A-K. Um – 'K' for Kerzak? That's my last name." Looking slightly bewildered, the pilot waited a moment to see if there was more. "Okay, great," he finally said, "fine with me." He turned back to admire his shiny white plane again. "I gotta tell you – up in the air, this Lark's a total dream-machine. Kind of a clunker on the ground, though. She's so damn big. So yeah, I could use some help."

For nearly twenty minutes, A-K worked alongside the genial

pilot. All chatty, Doc volunteered more information. About himself: that he was a bachelor. "Whoever marries me marries my sailplane too, and somehow, that seems to slow the ladies down." Said he was the best dentist in all of St. Clair. "Also, the *only* one. Good work, low rates. Be sure to tell your parents."

About Pat Grogan: That he had flown in the Korean war and that he'd been decorated – "though he'll never tell you about his medals." Said the manager had one wife, one cat, no kids. Grogan, in his opinion, was "a prince of a man, the kind you can count on your whole life, no matter what."

A-K snagged on what Doc had told him about the manager's war record. He'd seen plenty of combat stories on TV, but never when his own father was around. No matter what part of the world a war was being shown on the news or in a movie, the old man immediately snapped the program off. This was one more sore point between them: he was positive Dad thought his younger son couldn't deal with the tough stuff. Shouldn't, couldn't. Thanks, Dad.

Now, following directions, A-K held onto the tapered end of the first wing. Totally engaged, Doc jimmied the piece in close, re-aligned it, then rammed the spar end into the notch on the fuselage. This stuff is so cool, the boy thought. Kind of like putting a box model together, only way more interesting.

Together, the two of them attached the second wing and then Doc shoved in the central pin to hold it. By now, the Super Cub had taken off, pulling Grogan and that city guy up in the glider. Doc and A-K shaded their eyes, watching the two planes grow smaller and then even smaller, until they were almost dots. Watching the tow, Dr. Kingsbury let out a loud, appreciative whistle.

"Sir," A-K asked, feeling bolder now, "What's the difference between sailplanes and gliders, if you don't mind tellin' me."

"Well, that's a good question. Let me try to give you a good answer. One difference is: in a strong wind, a sailplane goes a little faster. Because of its streamlined build, it has what's called higher performance. Tell you though, prob'ly the biggest difference in soaring is with the pilot. Some just have a special knack for finding lift."

"I see. Huh. Sir, do you ever teach flying?"

"Naw, not me. Frankly, out of the office, I'm kinna impatient." The tall dentist suddenly cocked his head, looking pleased with himself. "Get it? 'In patient'? Today, I'm *out* -patient."

Dutifully, A-K smiled, as if he got the joke, which he didn't.

"No, what I like to do is fly cross-country, go for the distance," the friendly man went on. "Best thing about this new plane is havin' more room so sometimes I can take a friend along. When you find the kind of lift that keeps you up, say four or five hours, a person can get a little tired of himself. Least I do."

A-K went still. These planes could fly for four or five hours ? Without a motor?

"Truth is, it's gonna be a whole new ballgame for me from now on," Doc continued. "Just bought this fancy Lark about five weeks ago." Absently, he wiped his oily hands on his designer jeans. "Last plane I had was totalled."

"Totalled ? You weren't in it, were you?"

"Certainly not." Now Doc began taping over the seams. "It was one of my friends. Me, I'm real allergic to crashes."

Frowning, he added, "my buddy's a person you might call an accident waiting to happen. Smart fella and all, a swell guy, but the wrong personality to be a pilot. Reacts too fast, skips the details. Had two crashes with our Blanik before he finally stopped."

Uh oh, A-K told himself, that's what Dad says about me – "Too dang speedy". Well, maybe that's only with hokum stuff I don't much care about. I'd be real different in a plane.

By now, the Schweizer trainer had come back to roost and the gliderport was buzzing with people. Soon, another customer, a serious-looking lady with glasses, was being given her instructions for the lesson.

It turned out to be a non-stop day. Right after the lady came back from the flight, Ron towed up a thin man wearing gray sweats; then it was Doc Kingsbury's turn. A totally fantastic plane, A-K thought, watching the sun flash on its white wings.

No one paid much attention to the boy who kept standing there at the edge of the runway. But no one told him to get lost, either.

Close to noon, A-K saw a jeep-full of kids pull in, down at the far end of the field. The open car jumped to a halt right out in front of the big hangar that housed the power planes. Oh cripes, he thought. It was too far away to tell for sure, but the driver out there looked a lot like that Marko kid.

At school, everybody knew his dad kept a plane, one of those cool Mooneys, in the big hangar. They knew, of course, because Marko went around telling everybody. A-K tried to see who was in the small group. They were too far away, and anyway, he'd never be friends with those fancy kids even if he wanted to. Which he didn't, except for Tina.

Later, A-K helped Doc disassemble the glider. The dentist's flight had lasted over two hours! Said he'd found some great lift. Then, soon as A-K saw the current student was finished talking with Mr. Grogan, he said a hasty goodbye, with a promise to help the dentist anytime he was out here again.

"Mr. Grogan, do you have a minute?" A-K called, hoping the manager would remember him.

"Oh, hello, son. Gave you a lesson a while back, didn't I? Kerzak, right?"

His eyes friendly, the instructor went on, "Say, I just met your father a few days ago. Turns out he's joined a breakfast club I'm in, at the church. Did he mention it?"

"No, sir, guess he didn't." Now wasn't that just like Dad, not to tell him something helpful like that?

"Well, I'm putting things together here. Josef, the young fella in the hardware I've known for a long time, I come to find out he's your brother. Seems like there are Kerzaks running around all over the place!"

A-K shrugged, but secretly he was pleased. Back in Tucson, you only knew a few, close-up people. Neighbors, kids from your own school.

Briefly he wondered if the two men knowing each other might help him get a job out here. Prob'ly not. Dad wasn't a big friend-maker.

Naw, better keep trying on his own.

"Mr. Grogan, I guess you don't need another line boy all the time" – A-K'd been rehearsing this during the last half hour – "but ever since I took that one lesson, I've been thinking a lot about the gliderport." He grabbed another breath. "Wonderin' how I could maybe earn another lesson and see. I'm a lot stronger than I look and..."

Suddenly, hearing himself talking so fast, A-K just stopped. Slow down, he ordered himself.

"Sir, what would you think about my coming out here, kinna regular, on the weekends? Just be doin' stuff, well, stuff nobody else wants to do and..."

"Son," the manager cut in, "the truth is, our season's gone on longer than usual. Generally, we close down by the end of Octo-ber. For some reason, our fall rains have been slow to come this year. But they're coming, I can feel it."

"Yes sir, I know." The clothes they were starting to get at the cleaners now were mostly heavy coats and suits that smelled like mothballs. "But before the bad weather hits, well – " A-K went on, improvising, "take those rose bushes over there..." He nod-ded at the plants growing knee-high, alongside the trailer, then turned and gestured to the ones out by the driveway.

"No insult, Mr. Grogan, they look like great roses, but they need to be cut back this time of year. Also, don'cha think some-body oughta lay out some mulch for the winter?"

Back in Tucson, Mrs. Zaley, their partner's wife, had grown the kind of flowers that won blue ribbons in Arizona garden shows. She'd been like a grandmother to him. He knew something about roses, all right.

"Also," A-K went on, "I could chop down those weeds along the fence. Clean up some of the, ahh, the sheds. Made no men-tion, either, of the paper-studded blackberry bushes alongside the service road.

Smiling now, Grogan nodded. "Hey, you're talking like you want to be a handyman. Right?"

"Yes sir, exactly! And I'm real fast, too. Like, maybe I could answer the phone when you're up, doin' a lesson. I'd write everything down, an'..."

"Um hmn, I get the picture. Well, you're right, there are plenty of things that could be improved around here. However..."

Uh oh, not a good word, "however". A-K studied the flattened-out grass all around him.

"When we first met," Grogan went on, "you told me the family business was having a real hard time getting started. Right?"

Not sure where this was going, A-K nodded.

"Okay then, answer me this: Even if we were in high season – which we're not – how could you help your parents with the new business, keep up with your school work, and also, spend a lot time out here?"

For one terrible minute, A-K was speechless.

"Oh well," he improvised, taking a deep breath, "see, I only work at the dry cleaners, some of the time." He was itching to tell the manager what it was like to be around his father – about Dad's lousy temper, all the negative stuff.

A-K stared out across the field again. Can't do it, he told himself. The Kerzak family motto's gotta be: Don't Tell Nothin'.

Silence. Then, looking uncomfortable, the chubby manager shoved his hands in the pockets of his khakis. "Tell you what, son. I can certainly see you have a thing about planes, and bein' around them. Me too. Always have. But from what I've been hearing, sounds like your family needs you right now. Andy, admit it. You've already got a job."

CHAPTER 10

Leaning toward the mirror, A-K peered into his own hazel eyes. Then he glanced down again at the book open on the dresser. It was called *Improvement Through Self-Hypnosis*. Next to the book was a plastic water bottle.

"It takes a burning desire to change," the library book said. "*You have a burning desire to change,*" A-K told the glass. "And it's gotta be quick."

He flipped to the next page, and then took another swig of water. At school, he'd noticed, most of the "in" guys walked around carrying plastic bottles like this one.

"Ac-cept yourself," he read out loud. Then he told the mirror, "Ya better man, you're all you got."

Mainly, A-K thought, it's my attitude. My attitude sucks. I wish we hadn't moved out here. Big mistake. We were just doing fine in Arizona. I wish my whole family didn't look like we all just got off the boat. Dad and Josef, with those bony faces, lookin' all nervous...

He bent so far forward his breath made a little cloud-circle on the mirror: his thin, bony face stared back at him.

Didn't look nervous, though.

And how come Mom never wears stuff like the other ladies do, around here? Not even jeans. Just those kinna too-long dresses, and braids, on top of her head. Of course, she's real pretty for somebody old. God, I wish I was taller. Also, wish that somebody would write my English compositions for me. Maybe I'm gonna flunk out.

"Sheesh, get your act together, will ya, bud?" he said, breaking the spell. Shaking his head, he slapped the hypnosis book bam-shut. "Ker-zak," he said, turning away, "you got the attention span of a day-old gorilla."

People in town spoke cheerfully about its being an extra-long fall this year. Hearing that only depressed A-K, though. To him, what it meant was that he was probably missing out on all these great chances at the gliderport. The season was almost over and all Grogan had to say was: gotta back up your family.

Well, he did help. It just didn't show much. Hadn't he wet-mopped the shop floors after school last Monday? Yes! And swept up the back stoop, gettin' up Dad's gross cigarettes butts? Certainly had. Also, that time picking up all the trash out there in the alley, and a lot of the junk wasn't even theirs? Absolutely.

With no thanks.

Of course, Dad had had plenty of troubles, A-K knew that. Downstairs, late at night, his father kept going over and over his receipt books – adding stuff up, muttering about the bills, tossing down the aspirin. Then, really late, he would turn on the phonograph and play some more of that sad music he was addicted to: Hungarian stuff, violins moaning away. The ol' man played that stuff over and over.

Well, it had certainly been Dad's idea to start up a dry cleaners on his own. So who else did he have to blame? Not one single person but himself.

School was doing okay – well, except English. A-K knew he was behind there. Had an "Incomplete" in his workbook and he hated writing compositions. The truth was, working on a bunch of careful little words didn't interest him a-tall.

What he liked was action! But who with?

Some of the guys looked okay, yeah. After school, though, nobody invited him over, not even that line boy he had lunch with sometimes, him and his buddy. Seemed like most of the kids had been together since Kindergarten.

Fairly depressed when Halloween arrived, A-K decided this would be the right time to repair his red Condor. Can't go out trick or treating alone.

When he wandered into Uncle Harold's Hobby Shop that Friday afternoon, there was, of all people, Heck Judson, leaning up against the counter. No one else in the store, apparently – not even the owner.

"Hey, man," A-K said, trying for cool. "What'cha got there?"

Heck revealed a long, shallow box he'd just covered up with his arm. "It's just this model, an F-86. Thought I'd throw it together and give it to, um, to my little brother for his birthday." He sounded embarrassed.

What do you know, A-K thought. Another retard, like me. "Oh, yeah?" he said. "Looks like it's got about a million parts to it."

"Uh huh," Heck said, cautiously, "but I like 'em kinda complicated. So what're you doin' in here?"

A-K started telling him, briefly, about the Condor's crash. In the middle of his story, though, a white-haired man came wandering out of the back room to wait on them. When they'd both paid for their supplies – A-K had bought another roll of red tissue paper and three fragile sheets of balsa wood – the two boys walked out together.

"You wanna com'over today?" Heck said abruptly. "Show ya some of my masterpieces. Built me a whole bunch-a rockets last summer."

"Well yeah, I guess so." A-K kept his voice neutral. First time in this entire town anybody'd asked him over.

As their bikes rode crackling through the leafy streets, Heck glanced over at him once or twice. Finally he asked, "How come you aren't hangin' around at Grogan's anymore? Thought ya had the hots for gliders."

"Well, yeah, but I'm fresh out of money. Actually, what I'm s'posed to be doin' is working in town. My folks have just started this new business and..."

"And you're s'posed to be the good guy, right?"

"Well, good isn't 'zactly the word, but yeah, I gotta pitch in." Grogan's little speech still lingered in his mind.

"Hey, man, that's no sweat. Just quit sleepin'. Then you'd have a *lotta* time."

"Oh sure, and I'd flunk out of school."

Still, as he trudged on through the autumn leaves, A-K thought, he could change some things, like cut down on TV and listen to the radio only when I'm workin' at the shop. Also, soon's the rains come, I won't have to mow the grass anymore so there'll be more time.

Except by then, the gliderport will be shut down for the winter. A-K thought, frowning, so what's it's gonna get me?

When he arrived at Heck's house, he could see that the family was a whole lot more active and younger than his family.

To begin with, there was this pure-bred mutt named Boondoggle that tried to lick every square inch of a new person in the house – "To see if ya taste like a burglar," Heck explained, "so watch it."

In a weird way the dog reminded A-K of his owner: kind of gangly, like a whole bunch of boards nailed together too fast. Maybe an ally, too, if he decided to like you.

The mom, wearing a light-yellow jogging suit, was out in the living room, doing aerobics with some gorgeous babe on the TV. Mrs. Judson, who was small except for her front, had frosted blond hair and a toast-colored tan. She definitely looked like somebody in one of those physical fitness ads, an up-to-date mother.

"I bought some extra Halloween cupcakes" she called out, puffing as she continued her jumping jacks. "But lookit, guys – you get only one per person."

A-K noted that she didn't ask for the new kid's name, like his mother would've. Mom would've put on a nice welcome smile for the stranger, too.

"Thanks, Ma," Hector called back. "My mother's tryin' to get in shape for skiin'," he explained as they headed for the kitchen. "Whole family goes up to Mt. Bliss in the winter." Opening up one of the two pink bakery boxes, he handed A-K a cupcake – chocolate with white frosting and an orange hard-candy pumpkin, stuck on top.

Store-bought, A-K thought loyally. Mom always makes our stuff. But he wolfed the cupcake right down, and wondered if

Heck might try to wrangle a couple more for them.

Heck might have, too, except a boy, younger than he was but with the same white-blond curly hair, poked his head in from the back porch. The kid gave them a quick look, then disappeared back outside. In several seconds, he returned, this time with a small cherry tomato stuck in each nostril.

"That's my cute li'l brother," Heck told A-K in a flat voice. "Keep hopin' he'll run away from home but he probably won't 'cause he's chicken."

The brother, popping out the tomatoes, grabbed a cupcake, then imitated a dead-man's face for them. Apparently pleased with A-K's surprised expression, the little boy whisked out the door again.

Upstairs Heck's room seemed a whole lot like the hobby shop they'd just left. Stuff all over the place. Skiis and a pair of gray, plastic boots were propped up along one wall. There was a huge bike poster tacked over his bed. A line-up of rockets and model cars marched across his dusty dresser. Real nerdy stuff. A-K began to relax.

Picking up one of the hand-made rockets he said, "Wow, you've done some good stuff."

Shrugging, Heck dumped the contents of the new model onto a card table. Without looking up, he murmured, "Hey, anyone told you 'bout the tornado that blew away one of Grogan's planes last year, n'left another one in its place?"

"No kidding?" A-K shook his head. "Well, I knew the weather out here could get real crummy but..."

"Yeah," Heck went on, sounding strangely choked, "it happened, see, 'cause it was a *trade* wind !"

Groaning, A-K wandered over to a beat-up cardboard box at the foot of Heck's bed. It looked like the beginning of a crystal set. Impressed, he asked Heck, "Hey, you building this one yourself? All these pieces...man !"

"Yeah. Gettin' kind of sick of it, tell you the truth. I been fooling around with that thing for over a year. Don' know why I even started it now"

Heck got up from the card table and lifted the model onto the floor. After connecting several wires, he shoved the plug into a socket. A thin spiral of blue smoke fumed out from the back of the partly-built radio.

"Just s'bad as the last time I plugged it in," Heck said calmly. "S'pose it needs a li'l more work, right?"

"Well, you jus' gotta keep the faith," A-K tried not to smile. "Man, lookin' at all this stuff – you got a lot of hobbies."

"Yeah, guess so. My dad calls me a Jack-of-all-trades. Don' know if that's an insult or not." Then Heck, going back to the card table, started laying out more pieces of his F-86.

A-K prowled around the room a few more minutes, then found a batch of comics and a tattered copy of *Playboy* magazine. He sat himself down, cross-legged on the floor, and started to read.

"Whoops! I'm s'posed to start dinner tonight," he suddenly told Heck. "Gotta stick some potatoes in the oven, unfrost the hamburger. Almost forgot..."

"Unfrost, huh? Okay. So, what're you doing after ya eat?"

"Me? Not too sure. I've got this little nephew, Petey, going on six? My big brother asked if I'd take him out trick-or-treating for a while. Like a moron, I said yes." He reviewed how that sounded and added quickly, "But see, the beauty of it is, I'm gonna steal most of the good stuff outta his bag."

"Of course. Well, I'm stuck with a squirt, myself. My brother's nine, but I bet the li'l bums won't care. How 'bout swingin' by after dinner? Bring the nephew?"

"Oh yeah? Sure, guess I could. Like what, six-thirty, seven? When it starts gettin' dark?"

"Right. And maybe we could check out the school dance, after. What do ya think?"

"Okay with me," A-K said, trying not to sound pleased. Which he was.

Petey and Heck's brother, Lance ("Mom gave him that name after she saw his pointy little head," Heck mentioned) lived not too far away from each other's neighborhoods. But because Lance was older and he knew Petey was just in Kindergarten, no way would he walk with the younger boy.

Probably it turned out for the best, in the food department: with each one working a different side of the street, the two kids collected masses of candy and cookies in their separate grocery bags.

Even so, when A-K asked for one humble little Milky Way bar, Petey who was dressed up like a burglar (which his uncle thought was appropriate), offered to sell the candy bar to him for a dime.

Disgusted, A-K turned the pip-squeak down. For at least twelve minutes he wouldn't even talk to him.

"Listen, you guys," Heck finally said, "it's nine-twenty. Very late. Time to go home. You have enough stuff."

The night, lit by orange moonlight, had turned cold now. Frost could be seen on the rooftops. Dim, hooting figures were still out there, trotting along the streets with their loaded paper bags.

"Also, you're gonna make yourself sick," A-K added, giving Petey a bitter look.

"Nuh-*uhhh*," his nephew said, unwrapping another Tootsie Roll.

"I don't wanna stop," Lance objected. "No way! I got a whole lot more houses to do."

"Same with me," Petey chimed in.

"Hey, ya know what?" the tall boy whispered to A-K. "We oughta ditch these morons. Between 'em, they only live about two blocks away from here. All we have to do is head 'em off in the right direction. Okay?"

A-K thought a second. Lance was a third grader, Heck had told him. And as for his nephew, Petey had lived in the same house ever since he'd been born. No way could he get lost.

"Right," he whispered back. "Let's do it!"

After pointing out where the younger ones should go, the two boys sprinted away. Laughing hysterically, they ran in and out of a ladder-type scaffolding standing next to a brick wall, ducked into a cold, dark alley and flew out the other side. They dashed down Parkside Avenue and took a right on Spring Street.

By the time they got to the school, both boys were weak from laughing. And they were free.

"Dance of the Monsters!" proclaimed the long paper banner tacked over the gymnasium's entrance. "Bring your own ghoul!!!" Heck's friend, Boz Davis, shoved off from the far wall and ambled over, looking relieved to see them.

A-K quickly scanned the darkened room to see if he could spot Tina anywhere. When he decided she absolutely was not there, he checked around for Mark McCallister. Nope, didn't seem like any of that gang had checked in. Probably off having some big party on their own, only ritzy kids invited.

Briefly, his spirits took a nose-dive. Then he told himself, they're nothing but a bunch of snobs; *who cares?*

Listening to the loud dance music, the three boys drank paper cups-full of the PTA cider placed on a long, decorated table. Between them, they also ate nearly two and a half dozen of the frosted pumpkin cookies. Boz started on an apple, but quickly threw it in the trash, saying it was "too healthy."

Standing aloof at the edge of the shadowy dance floor, they nodded awhile to the pulsating CD music. The teachers had rigged up colored spotlights high on the gym walls that went off and on at different times. There was even some gizmo that sent out blasts of smoke about every half hour. Even so, the three boys criticized the dancing, the dancers, and even the music. After a while, A-K and Heck wandered out.

"See you tomorrow," Boz called after them. "I'm still waitin' for the girl of my dreams – ha ha. And don't lem'me hear of any garbage cans bein' dumped without me, okay?"

A-K was totally unprepared for the wild-eyed Victor Kerzak who met him out on the front porch. A-K had whistled nearly all the way home, in fact, feeling like a cool, with-it dude for a change.

"This, I cannot belief ," Dad began, in a hushed and furious voice. He ground out his half-smoked cigarette next to the several other butts that were squashed on the top concrete step.

Worried right off, A-K realized this was just the beginning. What was it Mom, the opera-lover, called it – the Overture? Ahhh man, – something bad was coming down.

"Ja! I was jus' going to call the police. Zat any son of mine vould leaf an innocent little child out there alone, in middle of the night..."

Innocent child? Petey ? Hah! The little twerp may be kinna low to the ground, A-K thought, but the guy's a con man!

"Dad, " he protested, "Petey wasn't alone! See, he was with this third-grader – my friend's brother? He was s'posed to get Petey home and..."

Oops. Wait a minute: now that he thought about it, well, they hadn't exactly talked about getting Petey right up to his doorstep. Just figured it would work out that way, it being such a small town and everything.

Oh man. End-of-the-world time. Yep, he told himself, I'm in for it now.

"Als-zo, your brother called. Josef's furious with you! Peter coming home in the dark, by himself. All zose hoodalums out there, jumping out, made him cry so much. Vun of them stole avay his candy, too. You knew you should take care of him. But no, jus' thought about yourself."

In the shadowy hallway, the gray-haired man all of a sudden looked totally tired of being a grown-up. Alarmed, A-K thought, Oh please, don't start to cry, Dad.

Clearing his voice, Victor Kerzak went on. "Vot you don't understan' Andor, ist there is much dan-ger out there. You haf been protected. You just don't know vot the vorld can be like."

"Okay, o-kay, Dad," A-K said tiredly. "Listen, you're abso- lutely right, I am a walkin' bum. So jus' send me off to juvie, stick me in jail. Anything. But c'mon, *please* jus' don't give me any more of this big scene."

His father didn't seem to hear him. Wound-up, the fragile- looking man started thumping on his own narrow chest. "Zo now, for the next two veeks, excep-ting for school, you must be vis us.

You are, how do they say it: on probation."

Probation? Like jail? Naw, Dad meant like being stuck at home. For two whole weeks?

Not even aware of shaking his head, A-K stared down at the floor. The flying season'll be totally over by then, he thought. And when the good weather comes back, Mr. Grogan won't even remember me. He might hear about this, too.

In a whole different compartment of his head, though, he knew the punishment was right. All that he'd been thinking about was himself.

A-K stole another glance at his father. Well, maybe the ol' man was kind of out of date, definitely older than any of his friends' fathers. But still, he had to admit it: Dad was right on this one.

CHAPTER 11

The early-morning cop, trying to be heard over the music blasting out of the Dri Rite Cleaners, rapped hard – one last time – on the store front windows. It was lucky the policeman didn't smash the glass, the way he pounded.

"Anybody in there? Hey! What's going on?"

A-K, who'd been cheering himself up as he worked in the windowless back room, finally heard the commotion outside. Turning down the shop's radio, a beat-up job brought over from Tucson, he hurried out to the front.

Both he and the uniformed man stared at each other through the newly-polished glass. Each looked surprised, wondering what the other one was up to.

A-K unlocked the two safety-bolts, then pulled the door open.

Inside, the young officer carefully examined the boy. A-K also examined the officer: large, red-faced, but the guy didn't look all that tough.

"You takin' me to jail?"

"Well, I'm not quite sure," the policeman answered. A slow smile started at the corners of his mouth. "Why? Are you a crook?"

"Not yet," A-K said. "See, I'm in here alone, doin' some work for my folks. This is their shop. It is zero fun. So, yeah, I'm thinkin' about maybe starting up a life of crime."

Trying to stay in charge of the conversation, the tall officer yanked up his left sleeve. He checked his watch and announced sternly, "Lookit, do you know it's only 5:17 in the morning? Can't you sleep or something?"

A-K knew he shouldn't, but he popped off anyway: "No sir, I can't. See, I got a bad conscience. Keeps me awake, day and night."

"Is that so?" retorted the officer. "Well, it is kinda refreshing having somebody actually admit they're, you know, rotten clear through."

The policeman, Officer Shawn Joseph Mulroney, second youngest of eight children, hadn't been able to resist kidding around either. But the next moment, he turned himself back into a professional. Must of reminded himself he was supposed to be the grown-up here.

"Listen, kid. This is just a routine stop. You might mention to your folks that we patrol Main Street twice, every twelve hours. Paid for by their taxes." And, having delivered his message, the uniformed man started to leave.

"Well, sir, we are all more grateful than money can, um, buy," A-K called from the doorway.

The big cop turned back and came close to losing it again. But, with obvious effort, he managed to stay serious. "Also, tell 'em it's great having our dry cleaners open again. About time."

Heading for the back room, A-K consoled himself: Yeah! Now that he thought about it, things could be worse. Lots of people were up working at this hour besides him and the cop. Milkmen, farmers and burglars, no big deal.

Now, accompanying the song blasting out of the radio, he hollered even louder than before:

Just truckin'
gotta keep truckin'
down that lone-some highway called life...

In spite of telling Officer Mulroney that he was fixing things up, what he was actually doing this morning was bagging clothes. Putting the cellophane bags over a whole line-up of newly cleaned clothes was a job that a slick machine used to do, back in their Arizona shop. But since one hadn't come with this business, every single item had to be wrapped by hand.

Not too many clothes left to bag: several floor-length party dresses, a pricey-looking dark blue suit, a man's suede coat, three or four blouses, some tailored skirts, and nice pair of dotted-swiss curtains. After he hung up a given piece, then bagged it, he'd reach up and hook the wire hanger onto the automatic rotator. It wasn't hard work, it just took time.

As A-K pulled another cellophane bag over (wow, look at this one, a gray silk blouse with sparkles sewn on it), he got to thinking about his mother. The blouse sure would look great with her silvery-blond hair.

Oh man. For the first time in his entire life he got to wondering how his folks must feel seeing all these ritzy clothes, six days a week, almost every week of the year, imagining the places people must go in 'em. All the parties, dinners in fancy restaurants, trips to resorts, to the mountains – had either of his own parents gone on a vacation – ever?

"Sheesh," A-K exhaled. He squinched up his face a minute, feeling real terrible for them all of a sudden.

By the time the folks arrived to open up the shop, A-K had made a decision. He hated it and soon's he said it, knew he'd start hating it even worse. But he did it, anyway.

"Mom," he said, "fix me up with a, like a work schedule, okay?" His voice was colorless, but he kept on. "I'm gonna start doin' some of the um, regular jobs 'round here? You just figure out what'cha need. Stuff, kind of like what ol' Josef used to do when he was growin' up."

Dad changed his mind about the "never" statement he'd made about the gliderport. It took a few weeks, but, watching A-K clean up, do errands and even be fairly good-natured about it, he relented. Some.

"So, you've been helping goot. Not raining today; vhy not go out to your plane field, look around. I vas young, myself, vonce. Unt, this's America!"

Pleased as he was, A-K also felt slightly irritated. How come his father always said things that way? So dramatic. Other people didn't talk like that. Still, he reminded himself, don't knock it. Sounds like probation's over.

CHAPTER 12

At Grogan's request, Heck took A-K through the whole glider procedure this time. They both understood that the new kid would be a fill-in, needed only if Grogan was desperate.

The whole deal only took ten minutes.

Disappearing into the storage shed right afterwards, A-K wrote down each step in a little flip notebook he carried in his pocket. "MEMORIZE TONIGHT!" he printed at the bottom of the page.

"Listen, winter's comin, ya know," Heck told him from the doorway a few minutes later. He looked puzzled. "Notice all that snow up on the mountains? This whole place's gonna be shut down real soon..."

"I know," A-K said, looking up. "But, see, I don't want to forget stuff." Heck got a funny look on his face, started to say something, but didn't.

While A-K did most of the clean-up jobs – picking up half-eaten Big Mac burgers, candy wrappers, sticky pop cans tossed into the bushes – the "regular" kid remained the one and only line boy.

Heck was everywhere, it seemed. He ran all the launches for the gliders and also hauled the returning planes back to their trailers with the green tractor. With his feet propped up on the steering wheel, Judson even ate lunch on the tractor.

King of the Hill.

It's fair, A-K had to remind himself. The guy got here first, done all this work...

But suddenly, on a breezy, stirred-up Sunday, in late October, Heck yelled, "Hey, man, com'on out with me, will ya? Ron's ready to go up."

All efficiency, Heck showed the student pilot, a bearded mechanic from Seattle, how to ease into the front seat and buckle up. Next, he connected the Super Cub's tow line to the sailplane's metal tow ring. Then, checking with Grogan who nodded okay from the back seat, the wiry boy pulled the canopy down over their heads. Standing at attention, Heck fixed his eyes on the revved-up towplane in front of them. Aw, A-K thought – gimme a break, Heckle. Quit showin' off.

"Hey, man," the line boy suddenly shouted. "Les'see ya run this one out."

Surprised, A-K dashed around to the left side of the trainer plane and lifted up the long, straight wing. Cueing from Grogan's signal inside the glider, he motioned *ready* to Ron Erickson up ahead. By now, he'd seen this procedure more than a dozen times.

His face was calm but not his feelings. This time, he was running the line! With a light breeze whipping up his hair, A-K ran with the Schweizer until, gently, the plane slid out of his right hand.

Not until the linked planes were sailing way above the giant poplar trees did A-K realize his head was still tilted up towards the sky. Embarrassed, he glanced around. Naw, nobody noticed.

His friend was right, of course. There was just about nothing to do at the field now that the weather had turned cold. Almost zero students. Still, if there was extra time after his Saturday chores in town, A-K hopped on his bike and sped out to the gliderport.

One afternoon, delivering a message to the power plane's end of the field, he fell in step with the Super Cub pilot who was heading that way, too.

"So, Ron, how much 'flying time' do you have by now?"

"Well, les'see. Counting my last trip up to the San Juan Islands, I've got about fifteen hundred hours in my log book."

"Wow, that's a lot! And you want to go 'commercial', right?" Inside the trailer on wet Saturdays, A-K had been listening.

"Absolutely. When I get me another couple hundred hours, I'm going to start applying around. UPS pays real good, for instance."

"Wow, but that's a lot of hours already! You got that much

time, just from towing?"

"No way! Listen, I have to scramble, trying to rack up the hours. Mainly, I'm only out here on the weekends. In the city, I teach flying, single engine. Also do some sky writing."

Single engine? Oh yeah, he'd read up on that. The small power planes. Cessnas and Aeroncas, ones like that. "Bet skywriting's a blast."

"Hate to tell you, but you sound like me when I was your age. Listen, this business is a whole pile of work, not a fast way to make money, unless you're flyin' the big ones."

"Okay, so, do you want to fly jets someday?"

Ron frowned. "Well, I don't know for sure. See, for the major airlines, you need four years of college to even think about applying. All I've had is a couple of years of junior college. What I'd really like to do is get on with a small company and fly commercial. That, or do bush flying up in Alaska."

"*Alaska?* Whoa! Which'd be better, you think?" To A-K's mind the adventure would be going up north. No contest.

"All I know is, you've got to keep on workin', kid," the sturdy pilot pronounced. "Unless your folks are millionaires, you're not gonna get stuff handed out for free."

"Funny thing!" A-K said with a slight smile. "I been noticin' that very same thing myself."

Except for Miss Olney's class, things were getting better at school, which was pretty important. His father had told him the minute he flunked even one single class, he could forget the gliderport.

Mr. Avery, the balding science teacher, assigned everybody a term project. A-K did two: one was making a weather station which he did, mainly, to keep track of how many flyable days there were in the late fall. Using dry and wet bulb thermometers, he also kept a thirty-five day record of climate changes.

"Wish more of my students had your kind of initiative," his teacher had said and surprisingly gave him an A minus.

No trouble in Hennen's social studies, either. It mostly involved writing down "meaningful comments" about the world news re-played on the classroom video. P. E. was okay too, because although A-K was a klutz at most sports, he was a speedy runner and the coach had misplaced hopes of luring him onto the J.V. track team.

English – well, that was a bit of a problem. He had mostly bad grades on his papers so far, but no out-right flunks.

Yet.

Tina Beckman was everywhere, seemed like: talking to her teachers after class, kidding around with her girl friends, forever speeding down the hallways, notebook and pencil in hand. Sometimes she gave him a smile and the local open-shut hand wave, in passing. Like he was one of her other zillion friends.

But still, he felt it was a little more than that. One rainy day, the green-eyed girl stopped in her tracks and confronted him: "Listen here, Andy, I think you must be playing Macho Man. It's cold outside! Bet it's 40 degrees today. So how come all you do is just keep piling on the sweaters? I've never once seen you come to school in a jacket."

He cringed, embarrassed that anybody had noticed – especially Tina. Truth was, and he'd rather freeze than admit it, the only warm coat he had that fit anymore was the thick cord jacket he'd gotten on his birthday. And the trouble with *that* was, the brown coat couldn't of ever been meant for a kid. With those heavy shoulder pads and wide lapels, he figured it was definitely for a grown-up. An old grownup.

Right after the family party, he'd taken it to school and shoved the coat way back inside his gym locker. If the folks ever asked, he could say truthfully: "Aw, dang-blast it. Guess I left it at school again."

Luckily his parents were so engrossed with their own worries they hadn't noticed that A-K's birthday present didn't live at their house anymore.

Now, standing up close to this sweet-faced girl, he asked himself, do I dare? Decided, *YES* !

"See, the real reason I don't need a coat," he began – then, noticing his voice was pitched up kind of high, forced it down lower – "is, 'cause...*secretly* , my chest and all my arms are covered with long, dark, hairs."

That stopped her. For an expert talker, the pretty reporter was speechless for at least a half minute, but then she rallied.

"On 'all' your arms? That's so – interesting!" Apparently working hard to stay serious, Tina added, "Sounds to me as if you ought to be in a – in a zoo. An-dor, I think you're wasting your time at our humble little school."

"Well, yeah," he said, thinking of his English teacher, "you're, uh, not the first to think that very same thing."

Finally, the day arrived when Heck asked A-K if he'd cover him for the last of the season. "My dad's all hyped up about gettin' up to the ski slopes now, thinks we oughta head out this weekend. New blanket of snow last weekend!"

A-K held his lunch fork in mid-air, listening.

"Not much of a job offer," Heck added, "the field's about to shut down y'know, but still, Grogan wants somebody to be out there few more times just in case."

Guessing that his friend might be afraid of being shuffled out of his job, A-K decided to ham it up (and also try to hide the sudden fizz that ran through him).

"Oh, yeah ? Aw-right, and when you come back, I'll probably be running the gliderport. Be making like eighteen thou' a year! They'll probably put me in the newspapers: youngest manager in the State of Washington. Maybe interview me on TV, who knows?"

"You get writ up, man, it's gonna be in the Post Office, under WANTED," Heck said. Not looking worried at all, he sauntered off.

But it rained that next weekend, and again on the following one. The day before Thanksgiving, Grogan officially shut down the flying operation for the winter.

All at once, Christmas was upon them. Having no pay job and therefore no money, A-K hand-made most of his presents. He built a wooden box to hold shoe polish and brushes for Dad, and a two-level wooden rack for his mother's cooking magazines. While he was at it, he amazed himself by writing out a gift certificate for Josef and Phoebe, promising five lawn-mowing jobs in the spring.

And since Petey absolutely, positively, denied having ratted on A-K last Halloween (explaining that the folks had found out but he hadn't told them), because of that, A-K'd made him an intricate, two-plane glider mobile. Small as the balsa models were, each about as long as a paperback book, they were probably the best planes he'd ever made, next to the red Condor.

"Uncle Ache-y, you couldn've boughten me nothing else I'd've liked as much as this," Petey cried. He had accidentally re-adapted his uncle's name once and realizing it made the whole family laugh, kept on with it.

His best presents were an AM/FM pocket radio, and a head-set to plug into the new radio. After he'd unwrapped the black head-set, A-K considered it a half-minute, then glanced up at his parents. They were both smiling, even Dad. A-K nodded and gave them a big grin back: yeah, I get it. Keep the noise down.

One other thing happened that particular Christmas Day, and A-K knew for sure he'd remember it all the rest of his life: at ten past four in the afternoon, Viktor Kerzak had himself a massive, heart attack.

CHAPTER 13

"Geez, Dad's sure been in there a long time, Mom." A-K complained. He slid down in the orange chair and shoved his legs way out. The two Kerzaks were the only ones in the waiting room.

"I know, Andy, but a heart operation's complicated." His mother seemed to be concentrating on her knitting; even so, she kept dropping stitches.

Finally, she glanced over at him. "Don't be worried, son. Our surgeon's done a lot of these procedures. Dr. Ned Neal, he's from the city. Very well known."

Mom was trying to sound cheerful, but the dark circles under her eyes gave her away. "An-dor, these doctors, some of them go to school for almost twenty-five years! Imagine it!"

Sure, trying to keep things upbeat. But she didn't need to be concerned about his feelings. Big hospital, the fancy doctor they'd hired, no problem.

"Well, of course I know it's a big-deal surgery," A-K said, "but I don't think it makes any difference if I'm actually here. In person, you know."

He slanted his eyes sideways, trying to check out her reaction. His mother frowned but didn't say anything. He glanced at the pea-soup green stuff she was working on. Hoped it wasn't a sweater meant for him. Kids at his new school, he noticed, did not wear the bulky, old fashioned kinds she made.

"See, um..." A-K shoved himself up straight and stretched, "I been thinking, Mom, now don't say anything yet, okay? Like, how about I buzz out to the airport and just kind of look around? I'd only be gone for an hour, hour-and-a-half?"

"I thought you told me the place was closed down now."

"Yeah, but there's always somebody out there." He waited a

few seconds, then went on. "Lookit, there's no TV on this whole stupid floor, least not for the visitors."

Silence. She just kept knitting.

"Also, I need something decent to eat! All's they've got downstairs is this mystery meat floatin' around in this gravy. Looks like motor oil."

Illona Kerzak shook her head. "Well, what do you expect? It's the day after Christmas. Son, why don't you look in my handbag, think I still have a few mints in there."

"I'm not exactly hungry, Mom. That's not the problem. It's well, this place is deadsville." As soon as he'd said it, though, he felt like biting his tongue off.

"An-dor," she said, apparently ignoring his choice of words, "this is a major operation. Your father's had chest pain for years. A heavy smoker, never exercises, worries about every little thing. Dr. Neal said it was surprising something like this hadn't happened before."

Inwardly, A-K groaned. It wasn't *his* fault.

"Now just settle down, please," his mother added.

A-K flopped over and stared down at his shoes. Phoebe and Josef were supposed to show up this morning, too. Maybe they'd trade places with him. In fact they should, in his opinion, but they sure didn't seem to be in any big hurry.

Worst thing was, there was absolutely nothing to do around here. By now he'd checked out most of the bathrooms and the drinking fountains on the first five floors, ridden up and down the different elevators, and found out the psych ward wouldn't let you look around unless you had written permission to come in.

He'd visited both the gift shop and the snack bar downstairs so often, the lady at the food place had started looking hostile. And, it still being the holidays, the stupid cafeteria was closing up in fifteen minutes.

A total bummer.

Yawning noisily, he plopped himself into the the chair and began flipping through a magazine he'd picked up from the side table. Mostly ladies' stuff, full of recipes and pictures of how to re-do your breakfast room. Leaning away from his mother, he hunted for pictures of good-looking babes in underwear ads but couldn't find any.

A-K had never had been able to whistle, so now, almost bored out of his skull, he started nodding, tapping his right foot to some tune of his own.

"Oh, Andy..." his mother murmured. He stopped.

From sneaking looks at her watch, he saw that ten torturous more minutes had gone by. A-K picked up another magazine and started slapping it on his knee.

"Son?" Mom said in a warning voice. "Stop it."

Whenever there was movement beyond the thick glass door that separated them from the long sunny hallway and the operating rooms, both Kerzaks looked up immediately. Nurses (and Mom said the cute one in the not-nurse uniform was probably one of the aides) came and went, pushing gurneys, hurrying along with charts, and rolling metal tables with medicine-looking stuff on the top of them.

But nobody, not one single person, came out to give them comfort.

"Listen, Mom," A-K said, lacing his hands behind his neck. "If I've gotta sit here, like, for the rest of my life, why don't you tell me about Dad's parents over in Hungary, okay? We're gonna start studying the Balkan countries pretty soon, in Hennen's class. Maybe I'll write a paper on it."

He was startled by her reaction: Mom whipped her head over and stared at him with this *expression*. All she said, though, was, "Call your teacher, Mr. Hennen, please. Show respect."

That sound in her voice. Sheech, grownups! "*Mr*. Hennen. But, like, Dad was born over there, I know that. And you weren't. Your folks were from the old country but you were born some other place, right?"

"Yes. In Switzerland." She kept her eyes on the knitting.

"Uh-huh. Well, look, Mom, I already know my grandparents on the Kerzak side are gone. But did one of 'em get what Dad's got now? A heart attack? What'd they die of anyway?"

Without warning, his mother plopped the whole project right down in her lap: two needles and the seven-inch knitted piece, still attached as if on a lifeline from the wooly ball down in her basket. Abruptly, she dumped the whole works, sweater and all, like: Forget it, I quit.

It surprised him. Here was his sane, predictable Mom, sitting bolt up like she'd just been electrocuted. Now that he thought about it, though, it was kind of funny how she always changed the subject whenever he'd asked her about the olden days.

"Moth-er," A-K pressed on, "I am prac'ly the only kid I know, who doesn't have any grandparents. Not even one. So tell me, okay? Your folks went to Switzerland after World War II 'cause of the Communists, right?"

"Yes, they did, thank God! They got out of Hungary in the late forties."

"Right, you've told me that. But what about my other grandparents, the Kerzaks? When did they escape?"

Now she went still. Sure, she must be a whole lot more worried about Dad than she was letting on. "Mom?" he prompted, "Hello-*o*, are you there?"

"Well, Andy," she said, taking a deep breath. "Even though my parents were old by then, they tried so hard to get to know you through the mails. Do you remember?"

He nodded yes. The Nagy grandparents who'd never had the money to come to the U. S. (though Mom had flown over to see them twice) died in Switzerland. Grandma Nagy had lived to be seventy-nine. They had sent him intricate, hand-made toys when he was little.

"Right! Sent us all those cool presents. And also your father carved those neat wooden ornaments we put on the Christmas tree every year. But no, I'm talkin' 'bout, how about Dad's folks?"

First time he'd ever thought to ask.

When he turned to look, A-K found his mother's serious blue eyes fixed on him. A nerve twitched on the left side of her high, pale forehead. Hey, he wondered, what's the big deal here? Had the Kerzaks been, like, traitors?

"Mom ?"

Bracing both hands against the padded armrests, his mother took a deep breath. "All right! You've finally asked me. So I'll tell you. And maybe it'll help you grow up."

That hurt his feelings, but for once he kept quiet.

"In 1956," she began slowly, "there was a Revolution in Hungary. Our people desperately wanted the Communist soldiers out of their country. You've heard about that?"

"Uh-huh, some." he said cautiously. "The Russians had these tanks and tried to take over, right?"

"No! Don't say it that way! What they did was *murder* thousands and thousands of Hungarians. Our side had almost no weapons, you see, not after fighting the Germans in the last war. And now our people had to fight off this new army."

"Dad was a real little kid, then, huh?" Cold all the sudden, A-K slapped his arms around himself to keep warm. He decided the crummy hospital must have cut off the heat.

"Not so little, but he was younger than you are now, yes. Your father was, ummn, just over twelve. Oh my Lord, son, they were monsters, those soldiers with their filthy weapons." Her voice was thick, as if she had a bad cold.

"After running over the cities, the Russians sent their murdering tanks and soldiers out to the little towns. The Communists thought they had to kill everybody who resisted."

Okay, Mom, he thought, staring at the floor. That's enough. Don't need to hear anymore. Stop.

"And our Freedom Fighters," she proceeded, perhaps unaware, "people like your grandparents, had very little to fight back with. Almost nothing!"

Sneaking a quick glance, he saw her face had gone all mottled with red in places – her cheeks, on her chin, the powered nose. That scared him even more than what she was saying.

"In your father's village, they were mostly farmers, you know. All's they had were a few guns, but not many, not enough: home-made clubs and pitchforks."

Pitchforks? Oh gods, this wasn't going to be like a war movie where you could just watch it and then snap off the TV and go get some ice cream. This stuff really happened.

Breathing through his mouth now, he forced himself to sit upright. "So, your parents," he asked carefully, "were they, um, in the same town, Mom?"

"No! They were from another village. They'd escaped a few years before. I've told you, Andy, don't you remember? I was born later, in Switzerland."

"Right, yeah. Sorry. Gets all mixed up." His mother was younger than his father. She must of been little when that stuff happened. And she'd never been in Hungary, just her parents.

He stared through the thick glass window of the visitor's door again. The long white hallway was empty.

"Okay, so then what?" he asked.

Massaging her forehead with one hand, Mom said, "You see, it was after the uprising had been going on for some time. There were bombings, small fires, big fires – so many killings." She stopped talking, took a jagged breath, then went on.

"This one night, your grandparents and three others, all part of the town's Resistance Movement, were sitting at the Kerzaks' kitchen table listening to a short wave radio. Your grandfather had managed to get one. Illegally, of course."

Suddenly she snapped her eyes shut, as if she'd ben there, herself.

"Yeah, okay, and then...?" A-K prompted. Got to hear the thing out even though he figured by now it was going to have a lousy ending.

"What happened is, the soldiers burst in. They smashed up the radio, first. Hahh-hh, God, that I should be telling this, but you asked me. And you're old enough."

She yanked out an embroidered handkerchief from one of her long sleeves, frowned, then scrunched it up in her hand. In this weird, singing voice, she went on: "And then, because of having an illegal radio, the next thing was... the Russians... shot... both your grandparents. Also the other three, besides. All five of them – murdered."

A-K's throat went dry. He had to swallow two or three times before he could talk. "Mom? Mom, it's okay," he whispered. "Listen, that's enough. I don' need to hear anymore."

What he wanted now was to just get done with it.

"Grow up, Andy," she said in a rough voice he'd never heard before. "Bad things happen."

Dad's parents, *killed?* His own grandparents. "Uh-huh," he said hoarsely. Now both he and his mother were whispering. "Okay. So where... um, where was Dad all this time? Like, with the neighbors?"

Agitated, his mother shook her head. "NO, not with the neighbors. Your father was there, too. In the kitchen. But don't you see, the soldiers didn't know it! He was on a daybed, in back of the family's huge enamel stove. Your grandparents had him all wrapped up in blankets."

"Wrapped up? How old did you say he was, Mom?" His whole self felt like it might – just – shut down.

"Almost twelve, two years younger than you are now. I already told you. He was in bed because he had the measles, the plain – old everyday, measles. It's crazy, but that's what saved my Victor. He was sick in bed! And those soldiers, they never even knew he was there."

"Cripes! And Dad was asleep, right?" he whispered.

Mom fisted her hands so hard the knuckle bones showed yellow under the skin. Her voice had turned gutteral; suddenly she sounded like a man. "Your father was not asleep, Andor. Better if he had been. No. First, he heard the, shootings..."

A-K took a shaky breath. "Uh-huh?"

"*Yes.* And he knew enough to stay quiet until the soldiers left. Your father had no weapons. He wasn't big. Probably like you are, now. Well, when he was positive they were gone, your father got up and came around the stove. And what he saw there, no one on this earth should have to... witness"

A-K had been taking just little sips of air for some time. After a quick, painful silence, he whispered, "Yeah, okay. So, how'd

Dad get away?"

Later, he decided, he'd try to deal with the rest of it. Just find out about the escape right now. That'd be better than the rest of this stuff.

Mom craned her head forward toward the glass door, as if she might spot his father coming out of surgery any minute now. Absently, she patted at her hair.

"You've gotten this far, Mother. I'm not a little kid. C'mon, tell me the rest."

She glanced at him, then looked away "Yes. Yes, I will! So, where'd I stop?"

"The escape. How'd he end up way over here in America?" Unaware, A-K started rubbing his hands up and down the sides of his church jeans. "And with the measles and all?"

"Yes, he was sick... luckily, it turned out, because that's why he was in bed." Now she was sounding tired. "Well: after the soldiers were gone, and he'd seen the bottom of... hell, Victor stuffed his mother's few pieces of jewelry and his father's sweaters into a pillow case. Oh, and some bread. Then he left."

"Left, Mom? With who? An' where'd he go?"

"With whom," she said automatically "Well, people helped him. At the first, he started out by hiding under hay in a farmer's wagon. It wasn't going in the direction he wanted, but at least it was moving away from his shot-up village."

A-K squinched up his face in disbelief. The ol' man, doin' all this stuff?

"After a while..." Illona Kerzak went on, ignoring his expression. "Well, mostly he slept in the woods, with other – travelers. Hah, that was a joke! Pretty quick, your father learned to keep his little sack of jewelry tied 'round his neck. Some of the people he met... even on our side... "

Mom rubbed her thin wedding ring round and round, keeping her eyes on the heavy, closed door.

"But, finally, he found a band of refugees heading *west*, where he needed to go. He was a very young person," she said softly, "but he made it all the way to Austria – can you imagine? And once there, he was safe. Took him almost a year!"

Looking close to exhaustion now, Mom thumped back against her chair. "He had to sell the jewelry, of course," she finished up in a tired voice. "That money, plus help from the Red Cross, well, that's how your father got to America."

The word 'brave' popped into A-K's mind. The ol' man's got guts, he thought. I never would've guessed it.

Minutes before Joseph and Phoebe arrived, Dr. Neal pushed open the heavy glass door into the waiting room. The operation, it turned out, had taken the entire morning. Dad's surgeon looked tired but pleased.

"Mr. Kerzak has come through a major surgery," he announced. "We ended up doing a three-way bypass and I believe it went quite well. Of course, he'll need some more time here, probably several more weeks, but he's doing fine." Mom leaned forward, her face tipped up to him as if looking into the sun.

"However," the doctor said, unrolling the sleeves of his green scrub suit, "the man's got to make some major changes in his lifestyle. Regular exercise, a healthy diet, and no more cigarettes! Ever! Main thing is, though – listen, I cannot say this enough – he's got to learn to take things easier."

Studying the two Kerzaks with kindness, he walked over and planted himself in front of them.

"Look: talk him into joining a fitness class when he's well again; that should help keep the blood pressure down. There are regular classes for adults, the nurses tell me, here at your own high school." Hesitating, Dr. Neal added, "Monday and Wednesdays I go to the same kind of class where I live in the city. Not a whole lot of fun, but I show up. Haf-to."

Then, as he heard his pager go off, the tired-looking man offered them a quick smile, opened up the heavy door again and started trudging back along the surgery hall to what was probably the next case.

"Take things 'easier'! Victor ?" repeated A-K's mother. She shook her head. "Why, that's – it'll take a miracle!"

A-K stopped breathing for a few seconds. Well, there goes the gliderport, he told himself. What that doctor meant is: Dad needs more help.

So forget the flying. "More help" means – me.

CHAPTER 14

Over the next few weeks, A-K tried to absorb what his mother had told him about Dad. It was hard to try and match up the tough kid his father used to be with this super-cautious, nervous guy he was now.

Still, for the first time in his life, he realized the old man had guts. Or used to, anyway.

Maybe Dad had just worn out most of his good parts trying to escape from the war. And then the troubles bein' an immigrant and all, a foreigner.

For sure, A-K was positive they were never going to be a cool father-son team like you hear about once in a while: Famous actor's boy follows in dad's footsteps! Or, like the plumber they'd had in two weeks ago: Mr. Wasserman had told them his son was his right-hand man.

"Someday," the proud father told the Kerzaks as he finished unplugging their stopped-up kitchen sink, "when he grows up, my Bernie will be taking over the whole business. Real smart kid!"

Well, different families, A-K figured. Still, to honor what his dad once had been, he offered to start delivering clothes on his bike.

"No, the idea is stupid!" Dad said without even taking another breath. "Lotta it vould end up on the street. Listen, Andor - jus' stick to vot I asked you for, okay? Nefermind the fancy stuff."

Even though his father'd lost about ten pounds from the operation ("the weight will come back," the doctor assured them) it seemed like he was right back to being his old, crummy self again.

Mom, who had overheard this brief exchange, cornered A-K later. "Son, your father's just had a bad day. Please don't take it personally."

Hah! he thought. My mother would defend a dog even if it bit her. She'd have some big story about how it'd had a bad life, probably starving. No, what Dad needs is plastic surgery on his personality. For-get him!

According to the chart A-K was keeping, the weather was a few days cloud-cover, several days low fog, and, usually three to four days of outright rain. Northwest winters...

Even so, on the weekends some of Grogan's old buddies, mostly retired guys, showed up regular at the gliderport. Passing around sugar doughnuts, they bunched up inside Grogan's warm trailer, pouring coffee out of his ever-hot coffee machine. His friends spent cheerful hours exchanging stories about their adventures in the air: hangar flying, as the tow pilot called it.

While most of their tales were maybe close to the truth, Ron Erickson had told A-K one time, some of their adventures got "flossed-up a bit."

Many of them had flown in wartime, but what they usually reminisced about was their peacetime flying. The happier days: planes they'd owned and sold, trips they'd taken, problems "upstairs," but how they'd always managed to find an airport to land in just in the nick of time.

The power airplanes at the other end of the field, not so dependent on the weather, came and went almost as usual. Parking his bike out the gliderport late one Saturday afternoon, A-K thought he saw Mr. McCallister taking off in the Mooney, but he wasn't sure. He'd noticed the low-wing plane out of its hangar once or twice this winter. He wondered what it would feel like to fly in a plane that had a real motor.

That Marko. A-K shook his head - seemed like he's got about everything a guy could ever want. So how come he was such a rat?

"You know," Heck infomed his friends at lunch one drizzly day, "it's gettin' to be real crummy down here now, but it's sure been great for the slopes. I'm tellin' ya - the snow pack's fifty feet deep a'ready!"

Then, maybe realizing neither of them had parents who would take them up, Heck added, "Either one of you creeps wanta go skiin' with us, sometime? My dad's got the rack back up on the Cherokee now; there'd be room for ya. Could rent your stuff up at the Lodge, and we've got extra stuff, too."

Both boys turned down the invitation. Boz explained he was saving up to go to a wilderness camp next summer. A-K thought of telling them that he didn't have the money because of taking a mystery girl friend out to the movies all the time.

Thing was, though, he knew they'd never believe it.

"Go out with *you*?" they'd say. "Bull. Nobody's that desperate." So he decided to skip that one. He told them another whopper instead.

"Thanks, but see, I'm still major-busy on the weekends," A-K told him, marching his spoon up and down the plastic lunch tray. "Nothing happenin' with the gliders, you know. But guys at the other end of the airport - the rich guys? - they keep offering me rides. It's real great, all those Cessnas and Sky Hawks."

"You wish!" Heck said. "Free rides to the booby hatch is all you're ever gon' get. Lookit, Kerzak, haven't you noticed? It's still winter."

Calmly, A-K scraped up the rest of his rice pudding.

"Oh, and remember," Heck added quickly, "when the ski season's over, I'm comin' right back to the field. Don't forget it?"

"I dunno," A-K said, stretching one shoulder, then the other "Got a real bad memory..."

After he'd unloaded the dishwasher and put the stuff away, he forced himself to go upstairs and start working on an essay he was supposed to write. Once he sharpened some pencils and was settled in his chair, however, he picked up one of the glider booklets he'd borrowed from the trailer's lending library. Told himself, I'll give it fifteen minutes then I'll do my homework.

As A-K skimmed through it, he came across this line: "Without doubt, it is the invisible forces of wind and sun that keep a sailplane aloft."

Staring out through his bedroom window at the black winter night, he repeated, "... the invisible forces of wind and sun"... man, that sounds so fine.

Slow as the action was in those chilly months, it turned out to be worth A-K's coming out. At ten-thirty on an early April Saturday, Doc Kingsbury came out and began putting his sailplane back together. A-K hustled over to help.

"Just gotta try this one trip," the bald dentist cried. "See if I can find some lift up there. And, hey - if you're free kid, want to come along? More fun for me if I have company."

As A-K zipped up his old jacket, he wondered if he should call home for permission. Frowning a minute, he decided, no. My dad was running his own show when he was littler than me. Guess I can make a few decisions on my own.

Besides - who's gonna tell 'im?

One of the trailer's weekend warriors offered to run the line for them. But, in spite of Grogan's towing them up higher than two thousand feet, they didn't get much of a ride. The wind had dropped by then, and the damp and heavy air lacked enough lift to keep Doc's sailplane aloft. The man and boy were back on the ground within twenty-four minutes. Still, to A-K, just that one, free trip up was worth every mile of the bike trips he'd been making out here since last fall.

In the new semester, he found he was in the same English class with Tina. Early on, she'd smiled at him from under her silky bangs, then, as usual, claimed one of the front seats next to her girl friends. After that, zero action.

A-K felt it was kind of a plus and a minus being in the same class with her. The minus side was, this was his absolute worst subject. As he described it to Heck and Boz, he wasn't interested in litter-ah-shure. Comics, yeah. Some detective stories, but not the stuff Miss Olney shoved at them. That, and also he was pretty sure the English teacher had it out for him.

Still, there was a plus side to it. Parking himself where he always sat, in the very back, he could stare at Tina Beckman all he wanted and not get caught.

He paid more attention to her profile than to the teacher. He was glad she kept her hair long. The main thing he liked though, was how she would look at a person straight on with those gray-green eyes of hers and not shy away.

Trouble was, Tina Beckman seemed to like everybody. It was good, in a way, but also frustrating. How could you get a girl like that to pay attention to just one particular person. Like him, for instance?

Sometimes out of class he saw her chatting with Marko, but it didn't look like a big romance or anything. 'Least, not on her side.

Sitting up straight, he tried to focus on whatever Miss Olney was writing on the blackboard. Dangling modifiers? Oh man, he thought. Just what I never wanted to know about...

Here was a surprise: on Friday after class, Tina hurried to catch up with A-K. She smelled like some kind of nice-smelling bath powder or something.

"Hey, Andy, are you still working out at the gliderport? Even in this bad weather?"

"Um, well..." he cast around, hoping to come up with some brilliant aviator-type statement, but he couldn't think of one. Shrugging, he said, "Well, not 'zactly, but thanks for askin'. The field's mostly clows nowd - I mean, *clowed*! Now."

She stared at him a moment, then put her hand over her mouth, so he wouldn't see her laughing. But he saw.

Quick, A-K thought - what was that line in the glider book? Com'on, brain - turn on! Tina likes writing and stuff. "Invisible wind?" No. Invisible "forces of - weather?" Nuh-uh, but it was close to poetry. "Sun and wind?" Swallowing, he thought, oh man, it was so cool what I read in that book, but I can't remember it now.

"Well, anyway, you're lookin' - good, Tina," he muttered.

"Chow."

As she'd hurried off, he stared after her. Half-thought she might sneak a backwards look before she rounded the corner. If she did, A-K told himself, maybe it would show - she really did like him.

Tina didn't turn around.

CHAPTER 15

On this particular Saturday, four men and a boy arrived at the grassy field hoping to fly. Several of them knew each other. Still, it was surprising they'd come out at all, because there was no spring fanfare to prove it was the right time, no dormant fruit trees suddenly exploding with flowers, or new-born calves bawling for their mothers. Certainly no warm breezes wafting around. It was too early for that.

These people came out today because something special in the air felt right: a strong, cool wind, steaming cumulus clouds overhead. Perhaps the invitation had come from that bright sun up there.

The four grownups came out in separate cars. The kid came on his bike.

Pat Grogan was there, puttering around inside one of the sheds. "Well, I'll be," the red-headed man said, stepping out of a doorway. "Live customers. Hey, lem'me get on the phone, see if I can get the tow pilot out here."

Several weeks later, still filling in for Heck, A-K stood next to the Schweizer, straight-backed, waiting for Ronvold's signal to raise the wing. The air was cold but "upstairs" the sky looked pretty interesting.

A weird Saturday, actually: there was this eerie yellow brightness in the atmosphere he'd never seen before. No ground wind, but Grogan had just heard a report of possible upper-air turbulance. Whatever that was.

A-K was envious right now: this sharp-looking Microsoft lady scheduled for a ten o'clock flight was probably gonna get a real interesting ride today.

As he waited for the woman to get settled inside the front

seat, a large, black crow flapped slowly off the top of the long wooden fence across the field. The boy followed the bird's flight with his eyes.

Now there you got one tough bird, he thought, stamping his feet to keep warm. Doesn't take off for little vacations or anything, no sir. Me and ol' crow just stick it out.

After the lesson with Grogan, the computer lady suddenly turned all girly. "Oo-oo," she said, patting her lacquered hair-do back in place, "it was just de-vine up there. I'm coming back, Mr. Grogan. You can count on it!"

Everybody, except the student, knew that Ronvold had only towed the young woman up to fifteen hundred feet. Had he flown the beginner into the light turbulance just above them, she might not have been so eager to return.

"Bad way for a new person to start, even with an instructor on board," Grogan remarked after she'd driven away in her little electric car. "Get too much shakin' around in bad weather, they might want to give it up for good." Then, checking his wrist watch, he gave A-K an appraising glance.

"You want a ride, son? You've had what – three flights? Think I probably owe you another lesson by now."

A-K hesitated. He wasn't sure if his parents knew he'd gotten these couple of extra rides or not. But Dad must know, bein' in that men's group with Grogan and all. No need to call the shop.

"Yes, sir! Sure do! Be ready in a second!" Breathing through his mouth, he dashed up the trailer steps to collect his logbook.

After calling over another pilot to connect the two planes and run the wing, Grogan installed himself in the back seat of the trainer. A-K climbed into the front. When the plexiglass canopy was pulled over their heads, the eager boy pushed as far forward as the straps would allow, unconsciously trying to help the plane move across the field.

The yellow glider rose up like a feather over a heat vent, lifting up, as usual, a little higher than the Super Cub's climb. In front of A-K were spots of sun flashing off the metal nose; on, then off, then on again.

A sudden, wild energy ran through him. "Oh man, this is totally cool," he whispered to himself. "No big ol' motor messin' up your ears. This's just ghostin'."

At three thousand feet, just short of Cougar Mountain, Grogan pulled the release knob and the heavy metal hook unlatched from the tow plane's rope. Up ahead, Ron waggled his wings, then dove away.

Using the hand-held microphone and head sets, the instructor repeated how to fly straight-and-level, make banked turns, recover from a stall. A-K spent most of his time watching the instrument panel instead of taking most of his clues from the outside. 'Outside' could fool you, he'd been reading, like if you're in a fog or messed up in a cloud. Gotta trust what the panel tells you.

"Jeem-miny Crickets!" Grogan exclaimed, once they'd flown away from most of the little towns below. "Take a look at Mt. Rainier, will you!"

For a heart-stopping moment, A-K thought the manager was talking about smoke coming out of the Washington's tallest mountain. It could happen. Not too long before his family had moved out here, another near-by volcano, Mt. St. Helens, had erupted, sending up tons of hot rocks and smoke as it blew about a third of its top right off. Killed a bunch of people, too.

But there wasn't any smoke coming out of Mt. Rainier. Something even weirder was going on: slanting off from the giant, snow-covered volcano were three long clouds shaped like flying saucers, each one angled away from the one above it. *Holy To-ledo*, he thought, looks like it's from outer space.

"Hey! What's goin' on out there, Mr. Grogan?" he called to the back. He heard himself using the formal name and, in another half-second, realized why. Up here, his very life was in the manager's hands.

"That's a meteor-logical condition, m'boy, and you don't need to shout. My ears work." Then, imitating the good-for-you voice of a tour guide, Grogan added, "They're called lenticular clouds. Un-believable, right?"

Half-scared, A-K tried to think himself calm: this stuff happens; it's happened before, it's gonna happen again. It's not the end of the world, just a – a weather condition, normal stuff. From the ground, you don't usually even know it's happening.

Seemed as if only minutes after he'd settled himself down, the glider was smacked by another gust of wind. This time, a bad one. Knocking around in the loud turbulence A-K tried to keep his eyes focused straight ahead but he couldn't most of the time. It was too bumpy. Now he wished he'd never agreed to step foot in the plane. Swallowing so often, he nearly ran out of spit.

Every which-way but down: it felt like the plane was totally out of control. First it slanted over on its side, then, hit by another gust, the yellow glider rolled over to the other side like a kid's toy bobbing along in a bathtub. After several more minutes of this, pretty sure they weren't going to make it, A-K snapped his eyes shut and waited for the end.

A minute later, though, it came to him that at least Grogan wasn't announcing disaster stuff all over the radio, like, "May Day, May Day" or whatever they do when you're in trouble.

Hesitantly, A-K sneaked a look out the left side of the plexiglass hood. Insecure as he felt right now, he was afraid if he moved too fast he might turn the plane over.

It looked as if the instructor was heading them toward a tree-less ridge. As they got closer, though, the glider suddenly started climbing real fast, almost like bein' in an big-city elevator.

"Hey, how about *this*?" Grogan yelled from the back.

Not able to turn around because of the snug harness, A-K popped his fist up and shook it. Yeah! If Grogan thought this was okay-stuff, it must be.

Breathing slower, he noticed the stick in front of him was being moved in different directions. As Grogan maneuvered the glider from the back, he kept them climbing, circling upwards. Pretty soon the front dial showed they had risen up another thousand feet.

Imagine, A-K thought, this plane doesn't even have an engine, and look at us, gettin' pushed up just by the wind.

"O-kay, Andy, let's see you take the controls," Grogan called matter-of-factly from the back.

Resisting a sudden urge to pee, A-K tightened himself up and went to work. He began maneuvering the stick and rudder 'slowly-carefully' as he had been taught. Hoped the stuff he'd been reading was still stuck in his brain.

Real choppy air! Even so, he felt he wasn't doing too bad. He kept glancing out of both sides of the canopy, making sure he wasn't flying the glider at too sharp an angle.

Gotta fly with the wind, he chanted to himself over and over. *With the wind.* Don't wanta lose the updraft.

Grogan worked him hard the next fifteen minutes, interspersing directions with "That's good, that's good!" and "Now, you're gettin' it." Finally, the instructor took the controls back.

They must have been up forty minutes by then. By milking more lift off Cougar Mountain, Grogan maneuvered the Schweizer up even higher. From four thousand feet, the snow down there looked like frozen ice cream.

And those weird, sideways clouds , what'd the instructor say? Lento, lentic-ular clouds. Yeah, totally cool.

"Mighty big winds up there, makin' those clouds," Grogan called up. "Pilot who can handle that stuff, well, I know a fella who took his glider up to thirty thousand feet! Worked his way up next to the jet stream. It's called flying the wave."

A-K narrowed his eyes against the bizarre sky. All these crazy winds, frisbee-lookin' clouds, he thought, gods, they keep you feeling out of balance, like bein' in an eclipse or something.

He shook his head. Don't think I've ever been so turned on. Kinna funny, 'cause the same time a guy could absolutely get killed doin' this stuff.

As they headed back, they circled down and around and down until finally, the field was in sight. Now he hoped Grogan might compliment him, maybe mention that A-K'd flown better than any of the other times. But, as things turned out, they didn't talk over this particular lesson again.

Not ever.

Dr. Kingsbury and his current girlfriend, a civil engineer, were waiting for them when they slid the glider in across the grass. "Hey! What do you think of those lennies, Pat?" Doc demanded as soon as Grogan had thrown back the canopy.

The manager nodded, his ruddy face crinkling up in a wide smile.

"And Sunday s'posed to be more of the same," the dentist went on. "Oh, listen Pat, why don't we fly in the morning? See if we can get some other guys to go with us? C'mon, it's been at least two years since we've seen such good lenticulars."

In the space of an eye blink, Pat Grogan made up his mind. "Let me put in a call to the wife. See if she'll cover the gliderport for me tomorrow. And we'll need Ron to fly tow. Wonder if he's free..."

"He's down there talkin' to somebody at the power end; says he'll be back in five minutes," Doc announced. Apparently confident that Grogan could persuade the tow pilot to help them out, the dentist started checking out the excited group gathered around them.

"Okay, so Pat'll be flying his Libelle tomorrow," he mused, "and I'll need somebody to fly second seat. Mei! My beautiful girl friend Who's-Afraid-Of-Nothing. Wanta come with me, doll? It'd be the chance of a lifetime."

The Chinese engineer smiled but shook her head. "No-oo, thank you, dear. As I've told you before, I find it's mighty small quarters in a glider. Anything over forty minutes, well, okay, maybe an hour, but anything more than that is too long for me."

Doc didn't argue with her. You could see they'd already talked about long flights before. The dentist's face began to resemble a blowfish from his efforts to stay calm.

"S'okay. Can't blame you, honey, it can be a long trip. Anyhow: let's say we've got Ron flying tow, well, then Heck, no, wait a minute. He's still skiing, so..." Doc's eyes wandered past the wispy-haired boy who was standing with them, then darted back. "Say! How about you, kid? You interested?"

"Talkin' to me ?" A-K was so surprised he almost swallowed his gum.

"Yeah, I'm talking to you!" The excited man laughed. "Why not? It's company I want. I'll be doin' the flying myself. Like to go to, maybe to the top of Rainier, but not much higher. That's just over fourteen, well, lem'me think, 'bout fourteen thousand, four hundred feet, if I 'member right. In my sailplane, it oughta take maybe five hours, round trip. You haven't had altitude training and I'm not nuts about the cold."

"Well, I..." A-K, much as he wanted to go, felt the need to level with the friendly man. "Dr. Kingsbury, I gotta tell you, I couldn't be much help. I'm still new at this stuff."

But inside his head he was chanting: Oh, please take me, please-please , take me with you.

"Hey, I'm not asking you to fly the plane, Andy," Doc retorted. "I'm doin' that myself; just want some company." The dentist flashed his large white teeth at the group, then looked back at the boy. "So, whatta you think?"

A-K's heart thumped so hard he wondered if anybody could hear it. Carefully, he avoided looking at the other pilots. Ron knew he'd only had a few lessons and the last lesson had been, just today.

Also, he was glad the boss was still inside the trailer, probably talking to his wife. Now that he and his own father were in the same church group, Grogan might very well know about the money problems Kerzaks were having. Even a quirk of those rusty-colored eyebrows might have shamed A-K out of accepting Doc's offer. But the manager was on the phone...

"Lemme uh, let me ride home and talk to my folks right now, okay? I'll call back in, Doc, hope you'll wait for me. Don't ask anybody else. Gimme an hour and a half, maybe two hours. That's all I need to find out if it's yes or no."

A-K swallowed convulsively. "Honest, I'll call you soon as I know."

CHAPTER 16

Mom was cooking wiener schnitzel when A-K got home, and he hoped this was a good omen. The kitchen was filled with the smell and crackle of hot, peppery meat. His father leaned next to the counter, reading the newspaper. He appeared, for him, almost peaceful.

Seeing that his parents were preoccupied, A-K tried to sneak a piece of the steaming pumpernickel bread that had just been sliced. Laughing, his mother caught him in mid-reach and smacked his hand.

"That's for dinner, Andy. You and your nephew!" she said. "I don't know which one of you is the littler kid."

He scowled at the comparison, but didn't mouth off. He knew he'd need her help if he was going to get the permission slip signed.

"Hey, you know what?" A-K began, " I just saw the neatest thing today, out at the gliderport."

"Oh, did you?" Mom said. "That's nice." She was busy stirring something on the stove. It smelled good, like some kind of a crackly meat sauce. Dad didn't look up from his paper.

"Yeah, no kiddin'. See, there're these real, weird-lookin' clouds goin' on right now – kinna like boomerangs. You can see 'em right out the window, if you want to."

While neither parent looked excited by the news, Mom walked over and peered out. "Hmmn!" she said, coming back to the stove. "What do you know. Very unusual!"

"Right. Grogan says they're some meteorlogical phenomenon."

Glancing up from his paper, Dad said, "*Mr.* Grogan, Andor. Show respect."

"Yes sir, Mr. Grogan. Right! An' uh..." A-K cleared his throat.

"I jus' got invited to fly up a-ways? Tomorrow? Just to get, like, a closer look at those weird-o clouds. Dr. Kingsbury – you know, our dentist? An' he's a real good pilot. Doc says he'll take me along with him, jus' a couple of hours. Grogan, Mr. Grogan, is gonna go up in his glider too."

"Going up a-vays, to *vere*?" Frowning, his father slapped the newspaper onto the counter. His thin mouth was already shaped around the word NO.

Ahh, why am I even tryin', A-K thought. I knew this's how it'd go. Still, he kept on.

"Well, just kinna up near Mt. Rainier, and Grog – Mr. Grogan – says he'd be totally glad to talk with both'a you. Whole thing would be just in one day."

His father shook his head. A-K pretended he hadn't noticed.

"See, Dad, these kinna clouds, they're real unusual and it's not like we'd be *in* 'em or anything. It'd be kind of like taking a sight-seeing ride. A few hours is all. Know what I mean?"

"Andor, in the begin-ning, you tol' me, you vere going to take jus' vun lesson, that vast all." His father spoke slowly, as if he were a very patient man, which he was not. "Unt now, look at you: planning trips – to the – *jet stream?*"

"Nuhuh, Dad, no one's goin' up that high! C'mon..."

At this point, he realized it would be smart to just drop the whole thing. Seemed like the ol' man had wrapped his whole grownup life around bein' super careful. Must have used up all his good parts when he was a kid.

And look at Joseph: too nice, walkin' around with his head kinna ducked down all the time, smiling at everybody on the street like he mighta done something wrong. My grown-up brother still calls our father Papa...

I'm not gonna be like them.

There was only one last chance, A-K figured. Impulsive as he was, he'd not yet told his father he knew about the war. About how great the ol' man had been fifty years ago.

"Dad," he said, swallowing in a dry mouth, "when you were a jus' a kid in Hungary, 'bout eleven or twelve, you sure had a lot of guts back then."

Startled, his father zoomed in on his wife, standing at the stove. Their eyes met, and held.

"I told him, Victor," Mom said in a low voice. "And it's to be proud of, not to hide!" Now, with deliberation, she snapped off the burner, turned around with her arms folded across her chest and stared at him.

"Ja?" his father managed. He looked, of all things, embarrassed. "So, Andor – I used to be brafe? But now I'm a – flop, zat vhat you think? Walk around vis jelly legs, 'fraid of the dark?"

A-K steeled himself: Ignore the way he talks. The ol' man's, like, camouflaged most the time.

"No, Dad, you're about the exact opposite of a flop." Now, he felt unshed tears run down the back of his throat. "Back there in Hungary you were brave as hell, except ya jus' don't advertise it."

There was a painful silence. The only sound was the crackling of spicy meat.

"Vell, it ist true," his father said in a voice suddenly thick with emotion. "Zat I had, that I found myzelf in the middle of hiz-tory, ven I vas even younger than you. And so you vunder, you think, when is it Andor's turn to haf something happen. Ja?"

"Something like that. Yeah, Dad."

"*Hmmph...*" The aging man took a deep breath, then asked, "An' you say it's jus' for a few hours, and my church frien', Mr. Pat Grogan, he's going vis you and Dr. Kingsbury, too? Zat right?"

"Yes, sir, flying in another plane, close by. And Doc, he's super cautious. Gliders n'sailplanes, they don't have motors – well, yeah, I already tol' you that, but, so there's not too much to go wrong, see. Fact is, when the guys get ready the night before? Grogan – Mr. Grogan says he'd be real glad if you'd come over for the get-ready part." He trailed off,"... if you wanna."

"No motor!" his father repeated, looking past his son. "Yust imagine how quiet. Mus' feel like – being a bird, your own zelf."

"In a way, yeah, Dad." A-K was tempted to get clever and say it was closer to bein' like an angel," but no jokes right now, he told himself. Don't mess this up.

"Vell, Andor," his father pronounced, like a king confering some great favor on a peasant. "Vy not!? Jus' a few hours, you said. Nice liddle trip! Ja – you should go. Then come back and tell us!"

Dad pushed himself away from the counter, dashed the rest of his coffee into the sink and strode out. In several minutes they could hear the low, emotional strains of a Bartok piano sonata from the living room.

Son and mother exchanged a quick, shy glance. "He'll eat after a while, Andy," Mom told him in a low voice. "You know what they say: the best and worst trait of Hungarian men is that of very great pride."

Also, A-K remembered from their partners' comments in Tucson they are "happiest in tears".

His mother began pronging the crispy meat out onto a paper towel. "This glider flying, Andy – I think maybe it's – growing you up."

Speechless for once, he thought of reaching out and patting the silvery-blond braids she wore on top of her head, the way you would with a little bird if the bird would let you pat it. He didn't, though, figuring it might embarrass them both.

"Oh, and I almost forgot," she said, clearing her voice. "Something came today in the mail. I put it here under the telephone book. I haven't shown it to your father yet. Perhaps it can wait a day or two?"

He pulled the letter addressed to his parents out of the envelope. Whoops! Attached to his mid-term report card showing an "Incomplete" in English was a note from Miss Olney: "Andor Kerzak: See me immediately after class on Monday!"

"Thanks, Mom," he said in a low voice. "Listen, I'll take care of this. Honest. I'll get it fixed up right after the weekend."

Feeling an extra heart beat, he thought, yeah, right after flyin' the wave!

In three more seconds, he was on the telephone.

CHAPTER 17

By 6:30 Sunday morning, Ron Erickson and the other soaring pilots who were flying Mt. Rainier had gathered at the gliderport. Besides Dr. Kingsbury and Pat Grogan, there were several men A-K'd never seen before.

One of them, a five-foot-tall Boeing engineer, was going to fly his new PIK 20 today. The fiberglass ship was already loaded into his aluminum trailer and hitched to his car.

Grogan, more eager than A-K had ever seen him, kidded the small pilot. "Hey, Blaine, see you've got your glider all ready to go. How about yourself, 'case you hit the big winds?"

"You're talkin' about rotor?" the engineer said briskly. "Yeah, heard there's some up there today. I been in it before. I can handle it."

Rotor, A-K wondered. What's that?

Ron appeared, as always, in his cowboy hat, carrying a clipboard. "Hi, kid, glad to see ya!" the pilot called out to him, jovially, as if A-K were part of the regular crew. The boy ducked his head and smiled, pleased to be recognized.

Early March. The fresh air was cold and there was a feeling of optimism among them, a quickness in the blood. Weather reports promised clear skies with strong winds aloft all day. He was also cheered by hearing the periodic shouts of laughter across the frosty field as other pilots de-rigged their ships for the trip over to Ranger Creek.

A lot of jokes passed back and forth, as if they were trying to pep each other up. Several of them kept checking out that unusual sky. Even Ron shook his head, smiling.

This morning it took both of them to take Doc's Lark apart — the glider was that big. And safe, too, A-K reminded himself.

Then, loading the body and the wings separately into their

trailers, the pilots hitched the long vans onto the back of their cars and trucks. One by one, they started a caravan – the dawn patrol, Ron called it – for the sixty-mile ride through the mountains to the Forest Service's small airport at Ranger Creek.

Yesterday, one of the pilots had complained, "Hey, listen, Grogan, how come we can't just get towed outta your field? Coming all this way sure seems like a waste'a time."

"Nope, my friend, you haven't got that right," Grogan had told him in a firm voice. "It's too far from here. The tow plane'd have to pull you up one at a time for over an hour to even get close to the mountain. That's too long, makes no sense. Ranger Creek's much closer to the base of Mt. Rainier."

Period. The group nodded and the doubtful pilot let it go. Grogan's word, about almost anything, was widely respected.

The tow pilot's final instruction was that he would fly the Super Cub over in half an hour, and the plane would be waiting for them when they showed up.

"Lucky we've had a little thaw by now," Doc Kingsbury remarked as he and A-K were driving toward the launch pad. "Lotta times in March, Ranger Creek's still snowed in." With one hand on the wheel, the dentist tried to shrug out of the puffy green ski jacket he wore over his two sweaters.

A-K reached over to help him with it, then yanked off some of his own outer layers. The clothes Josef had insisted he borrow, including the wool hat and gloves, felt scratchy, as if they were embedded with little bits of hay. Still, as usual, his brother'd meant well.

"From Ranger Creek," Doc went on, "it'll take us thirty minutes on tow, maybe thirty-five, to even get close to the Wave."

"Oh yeah?" A-K said, trying to sound matter-of-fact. What he thought, though was: thirty five minutes bein' dragged through the air? Sure hope the Super Cub has a real strong rope.

The car heater was going full blast and soon the inside air felt hot and breathless, like a sauna. He jolted along, half-asleep, and gradually the strange, fluorescent-lit scene of the night before came back: going to Doc's garage-turned-workshop with his father after supper, Grogan's arriving with the sectional charts, that skeptical look on Dad's face changing to actual interest as the pilots described what was ahead. Learning how to breathe into the mask with Doc's emergency oxygen tank, detailed instructions about how the parachutes worked. The whole thing had been like a part-detective movie, part-outdoor sport show.

A-K was positive if his father hadn't been in that men's group with Mr. Grogan, he'd of never allowed his son to go. Things sure had been fallin' into place this time, enough to get a person worried...

When they finally pulled in at the small grass strip, the redheaded instructor hurried toward them, his round face wreathed in smiles. Grogan, a bulky and freckled one-man reception committee.

"O-kay, so Ron's got one glider launched already," he told them. "And he's towing the PIK up to altitude right now. Yep, it's what we thought, there *is* rotor up there. But it's flyable. Just gotta pay strict attention."

Doc looked concerned. "Oh, yeah? What about flying around it, Pat?"

"You could, sure, but that means going pretty far south — no telling where you'd be if you had to land out. Also, you might miss the Wave entirely. Hey, you can handle it Kingsbury. Just keep your wits about 'cha."

One by one, all three raised their eyes and stared up at the eerie clouds stretched out above Mt. Rainier. Behind them, the sky was iridescent.

"Sure, we're tough, we can handle it, can't we buddy?" The dentist fake-punched the boy on the shoulder. A-K smiled back weakly, hoping he looked tougher than he felt.

For the next fifty minutes, they were absorbed in unloading the Lark's pieces and putting them back together. The pilots worked with even more finicky care than usual, checking and rechecking the moving parts of the gliders, going over all their assembly and pre-flight lists. Today was not going to be like other days, and they all knew it.

The emergency water, First Aid Kit, flares, matches, charts, and food went into the back of Dr. Kingsbury's cockpit. A-K's lunch sack was so much bigger than Doc's, he was embarrassed. That Mom: she'd even stuffed in a pair of extra ski gloves and a big ol' wool scarf. He thought of putting some of the stuff back into Doc's car, but he got busy and forgot.

The Super Cub's motor droned overhead again. Ron flew the short pattern expertly, then let down, landing once again on the frozen grass strip.

"Hey, Andy! Grogan says we're next," the dentist told the boy who was already seated in the back. Strapping himself into his parachute, the revved-up man managed a clamorous arrival into the front seat.

"Dr. Kingsbury, what does, uh, rotor mean, 'zactly? Been readin' about it, 'course, but jus' wonderin'..."

"Rotor, kid, is this big old hairy wind, is what it is. Happens with Wave, sometimes. When it's bad, you bang around like an old pair of tennis shoes in a washing machine. For instance, I was in a glider once that flipped clear over on its back, in rotor. There I was, hanging by my straps, upside down..."

Silence, then A-K murmured, "I see. Huh!"

Maybe aware of his partner's misgivings, Doc reviewed with him again where the rip cord was, and how it worked.

When the pilot was through, A-K cleared his throat. "Yeah, got it, sir. But like, how'll I know 'zactly when to use it?"

"Well look, kid: all of a sudden we're at altitude and I flip open the canopy, be-lieve me, it's time for us, and our parachutes, to say bye bye plane."

After a long minute, A-K murmured, "Yeah. Right..."

Methodically now, they reviewed one more time about how to use the oxygen. "We'll put on 'O_2' pretty quick if we get up above ten thousand feet," Doc reminded him. "I've got the tank up here in front. When I give you the signal, you place the mask over your face – remember how we practiced last night? Pull the elastic bands over your head; make sure the mask is real snug. Turn on the valve, way I showed you, start breathin' slow'n easy, then you're all set!"

With Grogan running wing, and Ron in the towplane up front, Doc's big sailplane started its take-off roll. A cold shot of fear went through A-K, but remembering the dentist's light-hearted tone, he ordered the fear away.

As the Lark rose up above the small airport, the altimeter indicated twenty-six hundred feet, twenty-eight, then three thousand. Now A-K could see snow and jagged rocks below them. All this wild country, he mused, most people don' even know about it. Wonder if that curling river down there would be a good place to fish?

Wonder if Tina'll ever find out about this trip. Man, if she does, then she'll know I don't just stand around mouthing off. I really do stuff, not like some of those show-offs that keep tryin' to impress her.

"Oh, and by the way," Doc called back, "keep watching for places to land – nice, flat, safe places. Just in case..." The altimeter kept winding on up: three thousand-sixty, three thousand-ninety. Then up to four thousand feet.

"Yes, sir, I'll be lookin'!" Half-scared, half-exalted, A-K peered down below. Seemed to him they were flying directly away from any nice, flat, safe places.

Dr. Kingsbury was listening on the radio to the other pilots talking about the sky conditions ahead. After switching it off, he resumed his conversation with A-K as if there'd been no interruption.

"Of course, in the air, you always have to be on the look-out, kid. That's your main job today – want you to be the spotter. Make sure we don't have any mid-air collision."

Good idea! "Don't worry, Doc! I'll be looking," he assured the dentist.

Rotor first socked them at 7,200 feet. The Lark was rolled over sideways, then – for A-K, this was the worst – the wind bucketed the sailplane up above the towplane.

Immediately, Doc called Ron and told him he needed to release – *now*, and thanks for the tow! Bang went the release knob. The plane, with its pale rope-tail flying behind it, banked off steeply to the left. The red-winged Cub headed down and was soon out of sight.

In the front seat, Doc was doing a whole lot of yelling; sounding happy, he cussed and let out rip-snorting shouts. "Yee-*hah!*" he hollered.

Like this was fun?

But, suddenly jazzed up by some crazy humor of his own, A-K called up, "Hey Doc, is it time to bail out yet?" He didn't get a chance for more jokes, though. In the very next minute they were slammed from the left side by what felt like an invisible fist. When the violent wind banged his head back against the seat, A-K groaned and closed his eyes.

All through the turbulence, the wind had a soft, high voice. Scary, almost like a crazy person singing.

Sweat covered his face; His inside tee shirt clung to his chest. For one heart-stopping moment, he thought they couldn't take any more of this stuff. Oh my God, please, he thought. Wings're gonna bust right off.

That reminded him of his splintered model and, terrified, he popped his eyes open again.

Doc was not tossing off funny jokes now. Seemed like he was just concentrating, trying to keep them alive.

With his arms folded against his chest, A-K could tell from watching his own moving set of controls that the dentist was having a hard time keeping the plane level. All he could do in the back seat was to keep his feet cramped up close together and try to make a tight package of himself.

Swallowing in a dry throat, he wondered if the rotor was usually this gross but was afraid to ask. He didn't want to sound like a wuss.

After what felt like at least an hour, the air attack up and stopped. Everything smoothed out. The altimeter read 8,900 feet. The sky was like a mirror, achingly bright.

"Hey, Geronimo! We made it kid," Doc boomed through the

mike. "Now watch us go!"

Something danced inside of A-K – a nutty kind of joy all mixed up with the gingerale-feel of cold fear. He had never felt so alive. Close to tears, he told himself: This's why I was born.

"Climbin' five hundred feet per minute, kid," Doc called back. "about time to hook up to oxygen, way I showed you."

Pulling the bands of his oxygen mask over his head, A-K shoved the apparatus over his mouth. At first he started breathing in and out too fast. It panicked him at first, even though he'd practiced it a number of times the night before. Finally, he got onto the right rhythm, inhaled the canned air, and breathed it out. In, pause, out, pause. He told himself: just keep it easy.

"Doin' okay back there? No air leaks?" Doc asked in his muffled voice. "Remember how I showed you?"

"Got it, Doc. Doin' fine. So, um, how far we goin' up?"

"Who knows, kid? Hang on to your teeth. Maybe drive this plane to Heaven."

A-K snorted. Oh man, I cannot believe this stuff, he thought. Totally amazing.

Barely northeast of Mt. Rainier now, they shot up alongside of the mountain as if the glider were a tiny, outdoor elevator. The icy, sunlit peaks of Washington State's tallest mountain glittered in the bedazzled air. Biting down on his lower lip, A-K watched a bare, rocky cliff drop away, lower and lower.

Only – wait a minute!

"Doc?" Suddenly anxious again, he thunked on the pilot's padded shoulder. "Sir, um, we're not goin' anyplace. I been watchin' this big old snow wall out there and it's staying in the same place except it's jus' getting more and more underneath us."

"S'okay," Doc threw back in his foggy voice. "The airspeed indicator says we're flyin' about sixty miles per hour. Also, got about that much head-wind, so we stay in the same place over the ground. With the wind against us, we don't go forward, we go *up!*"

A-K unclenched his teeth. Yeah, he'd read about that stuff in

the books. It was like Nature holding them up – and nothing else.

Slow, regular breathing, that's what they'd taught him last night. In-hale, ex-hale. Funny smell, oxygen, but neb'mind. Keep a steady rhythm. Breathe easy, don't fight it. A feeling of peace spread over him as he watched the clouds layering over Rainier. Headed for glory this plane!

With effort, he twisted himself around. Way back there he caught a glimpse of a shining Lake Washington, and the miniature city of Seattle. Then, leaning forward, trying to see around Doc's big back, he read the numbers on the front panel: 16,000.

Not miles, he needed to remind himself, feet. 16,000 feet!

What had Doc said? They'd stop above Rainier, but not go much higher.

A-K couldn't see any of the other gliders, though he wished he could. He knew, from the occasional radio contacts, they were out there. It made him feel safer having neighbors around.

The high, rugged terrain below them now was mostly snow-covered ridges, some spiked with trees that marched down into deep, blue-ish valleys. Way beyond, towering like overlords, were the other white-clad volcanoes – Mt. Baker to the north, Mt. St. Helens with its blown-off peak to the south, and Mt. Adams dead ahead.

"We're like – ghost pilots," A-K whispered to himself. "Up here, nobody can mess with us, all melted into the Universe..."

Doc must have heard the mumbling. "Hey, pard-ner, " he called back, "everything goin' okay back there?"

"Oh yeah, Doc! I'm totally glad you let me come along."

"Me, too!" the dentist said, shaking his head up and down.

A white sun glowed above them as if it were the first day of Creation. Leaning forward again, A-K read 16,800 up on the front panel. An unbidden thought came to him: I wish my dad had got to do even one thing in his whole life as neat as this. That lousy war, and now, nothin' but a smelly dry cleaner's shop that's goin' broke. Well, 'cept he's got Mom, and that's good...

"Hey, kid, we made it !" the dentist shouted. A-K craned forward again. It was true! They were levelling out at the top of this invisible wave of rising air: 17,500 feet, just northwest of Rainier, suspended in deep space, hushed – and plenty *cold*.

He'd told his parents he'd probably only get to the top of Mt. Rainier, fourteen thousand-something feet. That's what the guys'd said last night, but this was *way* higher. Maybe not mention numbers when he got back.

Dr. Kingsbury tacked them back and forth, banking slightly, hands light on the stick. Holding altitude, he continued that way for some time. A-K guessed this might be like sailing Lake Washington on a nice day, though he'd never been in a sailboat. Back there stood Rainier's white, rounded summit, surrounded by bare rock out-croppings, sudden cliffs dropping off into nowhere. His heartbeat sped up, then he chided himself: Quit trying to scare ya-self to death, Kerzak.

Chilly but safe inside the fiberglass cocoon, he day-dreamed of the kids at school, like Tina, and some of those big-deal guys swanking around in their letterman jackets. If they could see him now, flying up toward the jet stream, then they'd know *he* could do tough stuff too, scary stuff. Probably none of 'em would even have the guts to take a trip like this. Big loudmouths.

Maybe I'll tell 'bout the flight to a few kids later. Maybe Tina. Heck for sure, and Boz. Hah! Old Heck's gonna blow a gasket when he finds out what I got to do. This is *way* better'n skiin'.

A shadowy something appeared overhead. "Doc – is that one of our planes over there?" Now he remembered, he was supposed to be the spotter.

"Lem'me see – hey, sen-*sational*, Andy! Betcha that's ol' Grogan up there" A crackle of static, then Doc shouted boisterously into his hand-held mike, "Five Fox, this is Kilo Charlie. Five Fox, do you read me?"

Even leaning forward, A-K could barely make out what the other garbled voice on the radio was saying.

Brrr! Doc had just radioed Grogan that it was only sixteen above zero in here! A-K yanked off one of his gloves. Experimenting, he touched his bare hand to the metal wall next to the canopy; briefly, his skin stuck. Whoa – he thought, it's like bein' in an igloo!

"O-kay," Doc finished up over the mike, "Heading back to Ranger Creek now. We've been up an hour and forty; starting to get a mite chilly. Yep, my buddy's holding up real good, just like we thought. See you back at the airport, Pat, n'bout an hour. Over and out."

Just like they thought, huh? Neat! A-K smiled, wiggling his stiff fingers and toes. Yep, great trip up and a great trip back. Wait'll I tell the guys.

"I'm tryin' to skip the rotor this time," Doc told him, head turned sideways. "Also, it may be quicker gettin' us home."

He opened the spoilers, headed first south, then east. He descended down to 14,000, 12,500, then down to 10,000 feet. Watching the dentist pull off his oxygen mask, A-K did the same, then shut down the hissing valve.

At 9,800 feet, Doc remarked over his shoulder, "Sure better'n that circus we went through going up isn't it?" The white sun warmed them through the canopy at the lower altitude. It felt cozier and almost safe now. A-K closed his eyes; it'd sure feel good to take a nap right now, he thought. Got up so early...

A minute and a half later, without warning, the bottom dropped out of the sky.

Lurching forward, A-K watched as the altimeter started a rapid winding down, as if a spring'd popped loose.

"Hey Doc – what's goin' on?"

"Bad news! We've hit sink . Droppin' fifteen hundred feet a minute. Lord help us, hang on!"

They slanted downward, shooting past the east face of Rainier, heading away from the giant mountain. A-K had heard that most of the interesting glaciers were back here, but right now he could care less.

Snow sprayed fantastic ice needles off the top.

Doc frantically tried to read a sectional chart. "Doesn't look like we're gonna make it back to Ranger Creek." he yelled over the shrieking wind. "These crappy down-drafts...!"

There was a blare of yellow-white light coming up at them from underneath. So much snow.

"Na-ah, can't even make it over the ridge. We're too low, kid." The altimeter read 8,400 feet.

Then, over the radio, Doc began the international call for help: "MAYDAY! MAYDAY! MAYDAY!" Light-headed with fear, A-K felt his breakfast burning up in his throat.

"Help! Hey, help! This's Kilo Charlie!" the dentist shouted. "Going down, northeast side of Rainier. Five Fox – do you read me? Anybody out there? Over."

There was a thin, hissing sound from the radio, but A-K didn't know if anybody in the entire world had heard 'em. No time to ask.

Wind whistled past the canopy. They went sailing in, just above a dark forest of giant trees, aiming straight at a wide, open hillside of snow. Terrified, strapped in his narrow seat, A-K waited to be killed.

Doc skimmed his glider just over treeline. Lower, thick fir tree branches reached out and brushed the glider's wingtips. In the next few seconds they were free again. The sailplane bore straight down, aiming at an open snow field. A-K felt his bladder start to let go; except for a little spurt, though, he managed to stop himself before both layers of his pants got soaked. Wet clothes can kill you in real cold weather, he remembered. A hiking leader had told him that once on an overnight.

The white Lark landed with its black nose skidding up a snowy slope. Iced snow crackled and broke beneath them, making a loud, wrong sound like dishes smashing up.

For several terrible minutes, neither of them moved.

Numb, they listened to the cold wind howling down the slope. Even with the hood still snapped shut, they inhaled the sharp smelling firs and pines all around them.

"That was..." A-K cast around, trying to find his voice. Pulling off his oxygen mask, he cried, "Dr. Kingsbury, oh geez, you did so great."

"Uh-huh, thanks," the dentist replied. He didn't say anything else for what felt like a long time.

Then, woodenly, Doc started removing his gear. He got free of the seat harness and swung around, making an obvious effort to look cheerful. "So! How ya doin' kid? You hurt anyplace?"

"No sir, I'm okay. Fine. Listen, don't go worrying about me." He wanted to say more, to express his relief to this great, smart man for saving their lives. But he didn't. Kerzaks weren't easy with that kind of talk. Instead, A-K asked, "So, do you, um... sir, do you happen to know where we are?"

Peeling off his floppy wool hat, Doc started to massage his bald head. "Oh, yeah, I can make a pretty good guess. We're someplace facing the north side of Rainier. It may be on our charts, I hope. Only thing is, these hand-held radios don't operate below ridge line. And as you might've noticed, we're – pretty far down the side of this gol'damn steep hill."

Not moving very quickly, the dentist unbuckled some more straps. Then he leaned forward, apparently checking out stuff in the front. Finally he wedged himself around toward the back seat. "Let's face it," the pilot said, "Startin' ri' now, looks like you and me're gonna have a, have our very own, not to mention – free – Arctic Adventure!"

CHAPTER 18

Doc was ranting while he pounded on the stick. "Shouldn'a tried to beat-it. Gol'damn, that stupid downdraft! I could have gone west of Rainier, like the others. Everybody said go West, but oh no! Not me, Mr. Smart Guy."

Still strapped in the back seat, barely listening to the dentist, A-K thought: this's gotta be like landing on the moon. Bet no human's ever been up here, 'til us, so how're we ever... *NO!* Don't start thinkin' like that.

Bears around? Maybe. What else, wolves... foxes? Think they're afraid of people, 'cept in a pack. Bears aren't, though.

The wind shrieked, like a little kid's fear of witches. Clearing his throat, A-K called up, "Listen, Doc, it was the storm. You were doin' real good, 'til then."

"Yeah? Well, thanks for the vote, kid. Anyhow, let's get out and see what we've got here. Check out the damage."

Outside, the cold was shocking, so wild it singed A-K's lungs. Both of them took a quick pee, then shrugged out of their 'chute packs.

"If we're still here tonight," the tall dentist shouted over the wind, "this place's gonna be mighty slick. Careful how you walk, kid. Dig in with your heels. Ri' now I'm gonna see if we got tore up underneath."

Not too far down the snowy slope there seemed to be an abrupt drop-off, one that exposed bare, humped rock. After that, nothing but lonesome space between them and the next mountain.

For one sickening moment, A-K imagined the nearly eight-hundred pound sailplane streaking down towards the near-invisible valley hundreds of feet below.

"Hey! Thought the gear might be stove-in, but it looks okay," Doc's muffled voice called from under the glider. "Another piece of luck."

"Your landing wasn't luck, sir. Way you brought us down, – it was terrific. Nobody could have done it better." What was it they called it... shear? Yeah, A-K thought, the plane musta got caught in wind shear.

"Thanks, bud. Anyway, help me wedge the glider into the hill, will ya?" Doc asked, hauling himself back up. "We've got about thirty knots blowin' at us right now." The pilot's breath came out in steamy puffs. "Want to make sure this baby doesn't take off by itself."

The digging calmed him some. First he and Doc tried making an uphill, v-shaped trench by using gloved hands and their thermos cups. It turned out, though, the best way was by kicking into the iced snow with their shoes. When they'd finished, Doc and A-K inched the plane's single wheel into the frozen groove as deep as they could.

"Well, cold as it is, the snow sure isn't going to melt anytime soon." Doc stood back up, appraising their work. "Think this baby'll stay put awhile." He pulled off his gloves, shaking off shards of ice.

"One way to look at it, I guess, is, we could'a landed in that grove of trees over there. Would've messed the plane up real good, not to mention, us, and – whoops..." A violent gust of wind snatched Doc's loose cap right off his head and sent it skittering away.

"Hey, no problem, Doc. I'll get it." A-K sped down the hill, sure that he'd get the hat in a couple of minutes.

But he couldn't quite catch it. Though the floppy ski hat didn't move all that fast, it just never stopped. Breaking through the icy crust, A-K had to pull himself out of the heavy snow with every step. Breathless and up to his knees in snow, he finally quit. A few seconds later, he saw the hat bop down to the bottom of the steep hill they'd landed on. After another strong blast of wind it was gone, blown into empty space.

By the time A-K'd trudged back up to the glider, Doc was nearly beside himself with worry. "Lis-ten kid, thanks, but the hat's replaceable. You are not! Stick around, will ya?"

"Yeah, right," A-K agreed. 'Fastest feet in the West', his brother called him. Embarrassed, he nodded at the looming man.

Except, wait a minute: Dr. Kingsbury didn't look so great all of a sudden. His teeth were chattering and, from what A-K could see in the foggy light, the dentist's face had gone the color of oatmeal. Must be the cold.

"Sir, maybe you oughta get your hood back on," he offered. An image flickered at the edge of his mind: something from one of those outdoor-adventure TV shows about how you could lose a whole bunch of body heat from your head if it wasn't covered up. And this guy didn't have much top hair, either. Like – none.

"Yeah-yeah, you're right. Thanks." Carelessly, the dentist pulled his Gortex hood back up.

I'm not his mom, A-K reminded himself. But I sure wish he'd tie that thing on. No way is it gonna stay on in this wind.

"*So*, next thing, I'm gonna try the radio again and see who I can rustle up," Doc said. "Five Fox, somebody's gotta hear us."

A-K felt a little better, hearing the business-as-usual sound in the pilot's voice. Still, they'd been the last ones to leave the field today. Wonder if – no, he decided not to ask.

"O-kay, pardner," the dentist said, "your next job is to side-step up to the trees. Find us a place to get away from this blasted wind, 'case we don't... get found, right off. Yeah! And I'll try to catch somebody on the radio."

Clutching his gloves in one hand, Doc climbed back into the snow-bound glider.

The matter-of-fact way Doc talked calmed A-K some. Sure, they could hack it. This stuff must have happened to other glider pilots at different times. Flyin' around with no motors, whatta you expect?

More cautious now, A-K chunked out his steps, one by one, across the slickest part of the hill. The walking was better when he made it up to the grove of trees. At least in here your footprints left a mark.

It was quieter, too. Even though there wasn't so much wind, the tops of the small trees looked scraggly and bent over. Gotta be some humongous storms up here, he thought. The pines smell good, though.

As he ducked under the wispy branches, A-K saw a well at the base of a group of young trees, a deep, blueish indentation. Okay, he decided, we can make us a camp in here if we have to. Unpack the parachutes, use one of 'em for a floor, maybe swing the other one over all that brambly stuff, sorta like a tent.

Gods, he thought, we may be here awhile.

Before they left, Dr. Kingsbury had mentioned he'd brought along a pocket knife. "Soaring days, I always do, just in case," he'd said.

Lucky, 'cause we may need it, the boy thought.

"Sir, could you reach anybody?" A-K called when he'd inched his way back to the glider. Nice of Doc to have left the canopy open for him – but not a good idea. So dang cold!

Shivering, A-K nestled into the Lark's back seat, rolled the frosted plexiglass over them, and sat there awhile catching his breath.

No comments from the front. The dentist must be working

out a plan for them, he thought. Doc's a real smart guy; he'll know what to do. Humbly, A-K kept quiet.

The wind outside made a crying sound like the voice of a lost child. After five or ten minutes, and scared of his own thoughts, A-K needed to talk.

"Man! I'd sure hate to be listenin' to that noise in the dark, 'less I knew what it was," he announced. "Sounds like it's out of a horror movie, doesn't it?" After rubbing his arms through the many layers he had on, he clapped his ski mitts together, trying to hustle up the circulation.

Silence.

"Doc, um, you gettin' anybody?" A-K bent way forward. But the pilot wasn't working the radio at all. He was sitting up, but his head was hanging sort of crooked, and his eyelids seemed to be half shut. The red jacket hood was down around his neck again, too, not doing one bit of good.

Had the guy gone bonkers? Frightened, A-K poked him in the back.

"Doc ?" he repeated.

"Nhuh. Uhhm."

What'd that mean? "No"? No what? Scared now, A-K leaned forward and yelled, "Did'ja get anybody? Cripes, Doc, are you all right?"

Another long pause. Then Doc slurred, "N'good."

Fighting panic, A-K crammed his upper body clear around the leatherette front seat, trying to get a look at him. The man was trembling like a... wet dog.

"Hey, sir! Contact any of our guys?" A-K shouted rudely. Nothing. Still not willing to deal with what he was most scared of – that the only grownup around here was out of it – A-K rattled on. "Lookit, Doc, I think we better pack up, pronto. Get us some shelter. Be warmer up in those trees..."

"Don' – feel 'zackly too, uh..." Doc wheezed out.

The pilot was shaking all over. Must be, what did they call it? Shock. From the landing? Maybe it was just bein' real cold.

Cold: Right. There's some big-doctor word about how a lotta

cold can mess up your head, he remembered. And the wind had blown away the man's hat...

"Sir, you're gon' be fine. Once you get movin', you'll be back to – normal." His voice got louder. "So let's pick up our stuff. Doc, pay attention! We need our food'n the parachutes."

A-K grabbed what supplies he could handle for the first trip, rolled the plexiglass over again, and hopped out. Trouble was, looked like Doc wasn't making any traveling plans.

"Com 'mon, Dr. Kingsbury," A-K hollered. Desperate, he dropped his load of parcels down on the snow, and urgently pulled at the man's arms.

Doc yanked away. His face was rolled up in a frown.

"Hey – you gotta get outta here," the boy shouted. "You'll freeze sittin' around here, an' we'll both die." Finally, after a bunch more cussing and yanking on A-K's part, the tall man lumbered out of the glider.

"Good job, yep, that's it, that's it. Now – grab up your chute, Doc, and I'll get my stuff. Man, we gotta move."

The sky's getting darker by the minute, A-K warned himself. Don't show him you're scared. Try to act natural.

The dentist lunged across the slanted snow field. He grumbled, dropped his 'chute pack, picked it back up and then dropped his lunch bag. With A-K's support, though, he finally made it up to the little grove of trees.

More comfortable with deciding things now, A-K announced, "Sit down here, sir. I'll get us all fixed up. Don't worry." He straightened out the strings of Doc's hood, tied another little bow, and sat the man down on a half-rotted log.

After catching his breath, A-K began tamping down the snow in between the trees he'd chosen until he'd made a sort of floor. He crunched out a space about as wide and long as a car on the lee side of the big fir, and wedged in several fallen branches at right angles against the low limbs of the tree.

"Did this once before in Arizona," he told Doc, panting from his efforts. "Up in the mountains, ya know, with a bunch of Scouts? Funny – at the time, I thought it was a kick."

The hardest part was managing the parachutes. The first one kept billowing up like a giant balloon, then collapsed. Doc was supposed to hold onto one end but he didn't seem to have the concentration. Finally, A-K coiled the top shroud lines into a deep loop the way he'd seen jumpers do at the skyport next to Grogan's place. After a windy fight the chute spread itself down, quivering onto the snow.

He dragged the silky parachute over to the little hollow and lined the snow floor with it. To keep it there, he argued Doc into plunking himself down on top of it. Just as he started to work with the shrouds of the second chute, A-K heard something so amazing and so wonderful he could scarcely believe it.

An airplane! *They were saved!* Dropping the parachute, A-K sprinted, slipped, then slowed down and crunched with cautious steps across the two hundred feet up to the clearing.

Overhead was a single-engine plane, the same vague color as the long cirrus cloud behind it. Was it a search party? Could the pilot see a white plane on white snow? It circled, headed off for another area of the mountain, then sounded as if it was coming back.

Find the flares. Hurry-hurry-hurry. Oh man, he thought, why didn't I bring one of the flares out here?

"Idiot," he called himself. "Should'a thought of it. Gotta get 'em." A-K fell and slid back toward the half-completed shelter, then stopped in his tracks at what he saw. Inside the tamped-down burrow, Doc looked like nothin' but an old sack of laundry. He was either asleep or – dead.

"HEY! *Wake up, Doc*," A-K yelled. "Ya gotta help me!"

"G'way," the pilot muttered thickly. A-K moved closer, pre-pared to do CPR, but it turned out it was the ol' guy's mind, not his heart, that was messed up.

"Oh, lis-ten, Doc. Man, don't go nuts on me."

Screwing up his face, the pilot gestured vaguely but some-how couldn't get out the right words. Then, all at once, there was only the eerie, high-pitched sound of a hurling wind.

The search plane, if that's what it had been, was gone. Now

A-K felt as if he and Doc had just been erased off the earth. He thought how nice it'd be to slide into the silky nest he had made and go to sleep. It would be so nice and easy, and a zillion times warmer than standin' around in this cruddy storm.

The idea of sleep was close to irresistible, except, poised on the tight-crusted snow, he reminded himself: *Hey*, my life's just started. I've never driven a car, never been to Yosemite or New York, never played poker. Haven't kissed even one girl yet. Mom for sure would fall apart. And Dad, well, he's always about to fall apart.

This'd just make it worse. Really *really* worse.

He stared down at the graying snow. Okay, turn on your brain, Kerzak. What's that rescue stuff you been readin'?

The Civil Air Patrol. Sure! They're a huge deal. Pilots go down, CAP's gotta find 'em. Might have been what that plane was doing overhead. Lookin' for us. Bet so. What we got to do is stay alive 'til they get here, that's all.

They don't lose people. They're not allowed to.

By now, he knew the only grownup in the crowd wasn't much more use than a downtown drunk, so he went to work collecting branches for a shelter

Once he'd found what he needed, he shoved the longer branches in, filling in gaps. Then, grabbing the top of the stakes, he punched them down into the snow.

After checking again that the Doctor was still breathing, A-K looped the second parachute up and over the small tree-stakes, like a tent, then stomped five of the hanging shrouds deep into the frozen snow with his boots.

He wondered if they'd dare try a fire, but decided not to, because of the wind. Waste of matches.

When both of them were finally down inside the shelter, A-K realized most of his clothes were soaked. Instantly alert, he warned himself: if our body temps drop much more, we're gonna turn into a pair of stiffs.

Quick, how about Doc? Worried about frostbite, he jammed his hand under the dentist's heavy Pendleton again. "Dr.

Kingsbury, I'm not getting fresh," he said hoarsely, "jus' check-ing ya out." The dentist felt cool but not totally cold. And, seemed like most of his clothes still felt dry.

But for himself, not so good. A-K yanked off his wettest lay-ers, then dove back into the extra clothing he'd packed. Lucky, ol' Josef had suggested it.

He resolved then and there to quit making fun of his super-straight brother for all the rest of his life.

"Lunch time, lunch time!" he announced in a bright, false voice. Truth was, it was almost dark enough for dinner. Wonder what time it is? he thought. Doesn't matter, I'm starving. Should I put on Doc's watch? Naw, he might get mad.

Probably what the guy needs is a big hot fire. Try and build one outside later maybe, but not now. The wind's blasting too strong, and there's no dry kindling around. Tomorrow I'll try to find some hunks of wood and some thin branches.

"And in your lunch bag," A-K continued, feeling around "I smell... aha!... salami and mustard sandwiches. Also, I think this's a banana; little soft but that's okay. Taco chips, enough for two, if you don't want 'em all. And Hershey bars!" Guess this was how bachelors ate. Not bad.

He poured some lukewarm coffee out of Doc's thermos and argued him into drinking some. He ate both of his own peanut butter sandwiches, and four of the oatmeal cookies Mom had packed, saving three for later.

Right after, A-K realized he should of saved one of the sand-wiches for tomorrow. Dumb.

The caffeine revived Dr. Kingsbury briefly. "Helicop'er won' make it," he slurred. "Storm comin' – s'zose clouds." He wheezed loudly several times, then whispered, "Feel lower'n a dog." The cup wavered in his hand. A-K grabbed it. The dentist sank back and fell into a deep sleep.

Finishing the lukewarm liquid in Doc's cup, A-K decided from now on *he'd* drink the coffee; had to keep his thinking sharp. Give Kingsbury the cocoa.

"Now where's that stupid flashlight?" he muttered to himself. "Oh yeah, down here in Doc's gear bag." Hearing a human voice, even his own, was a comfort.

When he next poked his head out, he saw they were totally wrapped up in fog, or maybe clouds.

Gods, he thought, with Doc messed up, there's nobody to work the radio. Maybe there's some directions in the plane. And the fog'll be gone by then. We'll get rescued – we *gotta* get rescued.

"It was bad luck, Doc, that's all," he whispered to the snoring man. "Grogan says you're a great pilot."

Finally, A-K quit talking. Half-asleep, he suddenly jolted up, remembering the word he'd forgotten from that magazine he'd read: bet what's wrong with Doc is *hypothermia*. If it gets too cold, your brain shuts down. Doc's hat blew off right after we landed, an' he's got no hair.

In spite of his resolve, A-K fell asleep. He slept hard, as if drugged. He dreamed he was flying in soft rainbow clouds and that he was happy. Gradually the dream-clouds turned black and cold. Thunder crashed. Ice fell from the sky. Abruptly, he woke up and stared through the snapping parachute opening. Outside, the sky was nearly dark.

It didn't seem to be snowing. The wind was just as bad, though. He hated its high-pitched sound. Their tent shivered above them. How long had he been asleep, anyway?

"Doc – hey, what time is it? Dr. Kingsbury?" Silence from Doc except for a kind of snore-breathing, in and out. A-K hadn't really expected an answer.

He felt around for the flashlight. Beaming a small circle on the dingy man, he discovered the pilot had fallen over on his side. Taking off one stiff mitten, he unzipped Doc's jacket again, shoved his bare hand under the sweaters: yeah, still some body heat. He zipped the jacket back up and pulled the light hood on again. Tried to prop him up better, but the man's tired body was too floppy.

He checked the dentist's watch again – *wow!* 5:45. That meant they'd both been asleep for nearly two hours.

Wide awake, A-K admitted to himself what he'd avoided think-ing about before. We're gonna die up here if I don't do stuff right. Maybe we will anyway, but I sure don't wanna help it along.

He roused Dr. Kingsbury again and half-dragged him outside for another pit stop. As he stood alongside the groggy man, both peeing again, he thought grimly, the only thing hot 'round here is coming outta us.

Too bad the old guy isn't a fatso. Be doin' better right now if he were.

All the activity got Doc revved up again. To the boy, it was like having juiced up a Frankenstein – arms flailing, incoherent muttering. It didn't last, though. In just a few minutes they were back in the shelter. Instantly, the dentist flopped down to sleep again.

A-K'd never known how mean real cold could be. It spanked its deadly hand on any parts of him that were exposed. He dragged up folds and folds of the extra nylon layers to cover them both up. Then he crawled over next to Doc again. He remembered from some hiking manual that two people close together produce more body heat. Still though, he wasn't sure it was worth it: Doc's breath smelled real gross now. Yuck.

Afraid of freezing and wide-awake, A-K decided to try some positive stuff out of that hypnosis book: "You are sitting in a hot, bubble – bath," he chanted out loud, "steam – ing water's all around, lots and lots of steeeeam. *No*, here's what it is: I'm on this unknown island, draggin' my toes through hot, burn-ing sand. That's the way! And then these totally gorgeous hula girls show up, haven't seen a guy for years..."

The scenario cheered A-K up for some time. He kept telling himself: I gotta stay awake, in case a plane comes over. Got – to stay awake.

Another hour went by. Bored and lonely, he tried to sing some of the new pop songs. The only words he actually remembered, though, were Christmas carols. Bad timing.

He shook the dentist again and fed him a frosted Brownie. Remembering his survival booklet, he first shook Doc's feet, then

flexed his limp hands. Suddenly, coming to, the pale man reached
forward and snatched the flashlight right out of A-K's hand.

"Mine!" he said, sounding cross. Frightened of losing their
only light, A-K started to argue, then decided to skip it and re-
trieve it later. The guy wasn't going any place fast.

Huddled back to back with Dr. Kingsbury, forcing himself to
stay awake, A-K started to think about Tina. He remembered that
time she came to school with a black eye. Her and her Karate
lessons, he thought! Not trying to get by on just her looks. Neat
girl; wonder if she likes me? Wonder if she'd feel bad if she ever
heard I'd – well, died. He bolted up again. Geezes man, that's
sick-o! Turn off that kind of thinkin'.

Painfully stiff, he wondered how long it had been now? Two,
three more hours gone? He crawled over and peered out through
the flap. Blinked a moment, then looked again. Sure, terrific, he
thought, now I've gone nut-sy. Seeing spots before my very eyes.

Except, maybe, *wait a minute* – maybe there really is something across the top of that slope. He blinked a bunch of times to
make sure he wasn't imagining it. Yeah, the lights were still there!

So, I'm not imagining it, he told himself. Those bouncing
lights, they're real! Way, way over there, some rescuers are
comin'. To save us! Tears suddenly blurred A-K's eyesight; his
nose got all full. He didn't care.

"Doc!" he shouted. "Somebody's coming!" Silence. He fished
around on the parachute floor, shook the dentist as hard as he
dared. "Can you hear me? Rescuers are coming!"

"Huh? What'ja – whad?" The dentist switched on his flashlight. The light flashed for a moment against the billowing walls
of their silky cave, then he snapped it off.

"Hey wait, Doc! I need the light, right-now!" He grabbed for
it in the dark, but couldn't find where Doc's hands were. Sweat
trickled under A-K's arms in spite of the cold.

Abruptly, the big man hauled himself up and shoved his head
out through the little opening. So he had understood.

"See...noth-ing!" Doc announced.

A-K looked out behind him. Yep, Dr. Kingsbury was right.

All that there was was black out there, and the horrible cold.

"Rescue guys must have gone behind a ridge," the boy stammered. "Honest to God, Doc. I know I saw somethin'. Please, let me use the flashlight. I promise to give it back."

No response, like talking to a three-year old...

A tiny thump, then Doc muttered, "Hey, where'd id go?"

Something awful started pooling in A-K's heart. "Did you... sir, ya didn't drop the flashlight, did you?"

"Nuhhhn," the out-of-it man groaned. Now A-K heard the dentist thunk himself back down onto the floor of their shelter. Positive that time was running out, the boy felt all around inside the tent as far as he could stretch his arms. Nothing. No where. Gone. *Turn on your brain, Kerzak, if ya wanna' stay alive.*

Then he remembered.

The dentist didn't stir as A-K pawed furiously through the man's sack. Even though it was pitch-black, he managed to locate the four cigar-length flares Doc had packed. These might be even better than a flashlight.

They'd talked about how to light the flares, 'case of trouble. Last night, it'd seemed like just extra talk, the way grownups do all the time, jus' to show they know everything. But not this time.

He sloughed his way up to the top of the dim clearing. He had major trouble with the first flare; his cold fingers felt so thick and clumsy he could barely move them. On the verge of quitting, he suddenly remembered how they worked: they didn't need any extra-fine movements. Right!

Now he grabbed the end of the top string – what had the men called it? The lanyard – and tore it down the entire length of the cylinder, the way they'd showed him in Grogan's garage.

Panting, A-K launched the first flare straight up at the sky. The cylinder, arching upwards maybe a hundred and fifty feet, blazed into a long, red-orange dazzle. It didn't last more than fifteen seconds, though, and when the last of the four flares had been sent up, the night looked blacker than death. No sounds, no lights, but still he stayed on watch.

After that, no sound, no lights. Nothing. He and Doc were

wiped off the map. Forever.

He crunched his way back to their burrow and clambered in. Nearby, some big sissy began to cry. It wasn't until he pulled off one of his mitts and ran a bare hand down his own face that he realized it was – himself.

Back under the fluttering parachute, afraid of freezing, depressed, he stayed on watch. For a while he pretended he was a soldier, surrounded by enemy. Then, for the first time ever, he got to imagining how bad it must of been for his father. All those war guys gettin' murdered and not just the neighbors, Dad's own parents, and the ol' man never said a damn word about it. Didn't ask for one ounce of sympathy.

"*Doc*, oh my God, look-it!" he hollered suddenly, jumping up. "Wake-up, wake-up, they're comin'! I'm not foolin', yes...oh man, somebody knows we're here! "

Yellow lights slanted across the slope where A-K had set off the last flare. And it wasn't his imagination. The lights were real, coming up the hill like huge, glowing eyes.

Somebody *had* seen them. They'd been missed. People wanted 'em back!

The rough noise up there moving closer sounded like a bunch of chainsaws. They must be snowmobiles, but he couldn't tell how many.

One more time he trudged up in the dark, a dark he knew all too well by now, up to the only level spot on the white, crusted slope. Stone-faced, he waited at the end of a long, bouncing corridor of lights. And the lights kept coming...

Now he stood military-straight as if he, himself, had been in war. He yanked his shoulders back so far it hurt.

The surprising thing was (well, it surprised him, anyway), A-K felt this outlandish need to represent not just the two of them in this wreck, but also his own family, bein' as he was a son of a nit-picking, nervous, lousy-tempered, and... well, totally courageous Hungarian father.

Ron, the first rescurer, bounded forward in a silver, iridescent ski outfit, hollering, "Hi-ya, kid! Grogan's right behind me. Sure glad to lay eyes on you! An' also, where's ol' Doc?"

At that moment, A-K's despair started breaking apart like big old chunks of ice with the sun on it. The pain and all the gol'dam fear just melted away. "Down there a-ways!" he yelled hoarsely, pointing to the trees. He could hear the near-hysteria in his voice but he was way beyond caring.

Now all he wanted to do was just laugh his fool head off, keep laughing 'till he went near-bonkers. "Hey, and don't worry guys," he shouted. "Doc's got some hyper-somethin' problem, but he's gonna be fine, totally fine. I got him all tucked away in bed and – no kiddin', the man's jus' sleepin' like a ba-by!"

CHAPTER 19

In the first weeks after the crash and rescue, A-K found out one major thing about being in the media: fame was a pain.

For instance, right after announcements in first period English, Miss Olney rose up from her desk, nearly bursting with good intentions.

"Class!" she marveled, "as I'm sure you know, we have a brave young person in our midst, a celebrity, Mr. Andor Kerzak! Why, our Andy's even been on television. Did any of you see his interview on KOMO Monday night?"

Several hands waved up in the air.

While the teacher talked, A-K started sifting through his options. Throw up on his desk? Work up a coughing fit? Maybe hit the floor.

A crude noise let off somewhere in the room and that slowed Miss Olney down, briefly.

"Oo-oo, An-dor, save me, save me," one of the druggies called out. A-K slid down in his seat.

"Dear," Miss Olney said, ignoring them, "I wonder if you'd stand up and tell us what you thought about while you were, well, trying to survive on that freezing mountain top."

A-K panicked. Leave it to an English teacher, he thought. She probably hopes I wrote a poem up there. Oh sure, like, snowblow doe-dee-doe. Ahh man, I hate public speakin'.

Heads turned to look at him. A few of the kids looked sympathetic.

"It wasn't the biggest deal in the world," he muttered. "Not much to talk about." His main worries had been about wild animals that never showed up, the terrible cold, running out of food, and how to keep ol' Doc alive. Well – and, yeah, okay, he'd also thought about Tina a little bit but no way was he going tell 'em that kind of stuff.

"I'd like to see you stand, Andor," Miss Olney repeated, "so we can hear you better."

Reluctantly he dragged himself out of his seat. "Well, um, first we had this bad luck and then, ya know," he shrugged, "we got rescued."

"Oh, no, it was much more than that." Miss Olney insisted. "Why, two days after the crash, Dr. Kingsbury told KUOW if it hadn't been for you, he wouldn't be alive today!"

Just a few more of her flowery comments and A-K knew he'd be a social outcast. Finally he figured out to just nod and keep saying, "Yes, ma'am" or "No, ma'am."

It worked. Pretty quick the English teacher stopped acting like one of those hosts on a TV game show and let him sit down again.

One decent thing did happen in that first period. At the end of class, Miss Olney told A-K that if he wanted to re-write his first semester's term paper and turn it in by this Friday, she'd be willing to change the "F" to a passing grade.

"Yes, ma'am, I will. Thanks! And would you mind letting me do it about the trip I jus' was on?" Sure would be more exciting than the essay he'd planned, earlier: *Different Kinds of Cactuses to be Found in Northern Arizona.*

"Well, I was hoping you would, dear. Certainly. I'll look forward to reading it." For the first time ever, Miss Olney gave him one of her sweet gray smiles.

Wonder of wonders: Even ol' Marko had something nice to say for a change. At least, A-K thought the guy was going to be half-way decent.

"Way to go, Ko-jak!" the muscle-bound boy said, stopping him on the stairway. Per usual, Marko glanced around, hoping for an audience. "Hey, man," he said in a loud voice, "I been thinking about takin' some flying lessons myself. So maybe – can you gimme a few pointers?"

Kojak? A-K wondered if McCallister really thought that was

his name. Probably not.

"Well, I dunno. Like, what?"

There was only one-way traffic on the stairway now. Three other kids had stopped now, waiting to see what Marko would say.

"Hey, I wan'cha to teach me how to _crash_, man! Hear you're real great at it." Then the broad football player started fake-laughing at his own joke. No one else did, though. Not the guys, not the girl.

"Mark-o, get a life, will you ?" said the girl who was also a tenth grader. Thinning her lips, she turned and looked at the embarrassed A-K and shook her head as if to say: just ignore that creep.

A-K, who'd already chalked up two late demerits in his next class, took off in a hurry. Luckily (or maybe not) he missed the slit-eyed look the football player aimed at his back.

Tina Beckman stopped him in the hallway that same afternoon. Shifting his books, he grinned at her but this time she didn't smile back. Oh man, what'd happened to her face ?

All those bruises! One cheek was an ugly yellow and gray color and the skin around her left eye was real puffy. He dropped his eyes, not wanting to embarrass her.

But she didn't miss much, Tina didn't. Watching him try not to react, she reached up and smoothed down the collars of her white sweater. "O-kay, so how do you like my new look?"

"Uh, well, you don't actually... so did'ja walk into a door or something?"

"Gee, thanks ; it's that bad, huh? No, it was my sparring partner. You know Hetty Rabinowitz? Well, she delivered a whammo punch on me Tuesday night before I could stop her. My fault."

A-K nodded, seriously, like, what else would a pretty girl like her be doing on a Tuesday night? Of course: tryin' to beat up a friend.

"The training s'posed to teach you not to ever let your guard down and, oh, never mind. Let's talk about it later."

All business now, the purposeful girl asked when she could interview him for the school newspaper. She'd heard "some different versions" of the crash and she wanted to get it straight before she tried to write about it.

Different versions? What does that mean, he wondered. Geez, a crash is a crash. He shrugged, though, and agreed to meet her in the Science lab, Thursday, right after school.

Not too shabby, he thought. I'd be glad to sit right next to her and talk about, anything. Isn't exactly like a date, but still it's better'n nothing. Maybe, finally, I'll get somethin' goin' on Thursday.

"Y'know, the whole thing's been like, blown up," A-K announced, hoping to sound modest. He sat down next to her at the long black lab table. The last bell of the day had gone off and the school was almost empty. "The whole deal got too much publicity."

Serious-faced, Tina nodded, her pencil poised just above her notebook. Something was off – she didn't seem like her regular self. It was as if something else was on her mind.

How come she won't look at me, he wondered. Does she think I've turned conceited, all the sudden? Hah! The bad dreams I been havin,' almost flunkin' a couple of classes, not to mention all the embarrassing publicity.

His story had been in both of the Seattle papers, with a seven-inch column in the morning one. He'd hardly been aware of the photographer who'd arrived in one of the snowmobiles, along with the rescuers, but the guy got a bunch of photos. And now, a local reporter was planning an "in-depth story" of the crash and rescue for the town's weekly *Saint Clair Herald*.

"Oh we-ll, just can't help it when you're famous, I guess," Tina said lightly. Then her voice changed. "An-dor, now listen, don't get upset, but..."

Whew, women are complicated, A-K thought. This is just s'posed to be a little story for the school paper. So how come she's makin' like it a big deal?

"Listen", she went on, "somebody's got to tell you, Andy. Mark McCallister is going around saying *you* made the plane go down. That what happened was your fault. It's, well, you know – sort of all over school? A lot of people aren't sure."

"Wha-at?" A-K straightened up. "That jerk's sayin' *what?* He doesn't know what he's talkin' about! For one thing, Marko wasn't there. Number two, he knows zero 'bout sailplanes or gliders either. Where'd you hear that bullsh...shhh, baloney?"

"We-ll, he called me up two nights ago, says his dad – you know, he's a pilot? He said even though you were in the back of the glider, you had all the same controls as in the front."

Now she looked up from her notebook. "Is that right?" Tina asked, frowning. "Front an' back have dual controls?"

"Yeah, sure. All the two-seaters do." Unexpectedly, he had a fit of swallowing, his throat was so dry.

"Well, Marko's father says no way would Doc make that kind of mistake – deliberately flying into a storm. That Dr. Kingsbury has flown in bad weather for years and years, without ever any trouble. Never."

"Guess that's right, yeah. He's a very good pilot but, ya-know, sometimes even the of best guys..."

"...and, Mr. McCallister says it must of been you who made the glider lose altitude," she went on, in a trebly voice. "He said that even though you rode in the back, you had the same controls as up front."

Oh gods, he thought, what a load somebody's been telling her. And he knew who: Marko. Bet he's told that baloney to everybody, sayin' I messed with the controls. Yeah, a couple times flying with Grogan, in perfect weather, he's let me do some little stuff. But never Doc, never in his plane.

And never in a storm.

That muscle-head's had it out for me since we first met up. So now he's invented all this stuff, and told it to his father. Guess he's spreadin' it around to everybody. Dirty liar! Still, some people'll probably believe 'im. Family's lived here forever. Mr. McCallister's s'posed to be a decent guy, but he's sure got himself fooled here.

He flicked another look at her: the dark-haired girl was staring down at her folder. The expression on her face was like a question mark.

Terrific, he thought. So here's what the town thinks: the new kid, me, must be a liar an' probably not too bright. That the father's "not friendly", and the mother's "quiet...so, well, probably nothing much to her, either".

Oh man, I wish we'd never moved here! Maybe I'll just take off and go back to Arizona. The Zaleys like me, I'll live with them.

Only person besides me who knows what really happened is Doc. And I'm pretty sure he didn't do one damn thing wrong, either. Naw, it was that bitch of a storm. The wind...

He sneaked another look at Tina. She was still frowning down at the blank paper she'd spread out on the lab table. The late afternoon sun had just now touched her face.

"Tina, I'd appreciate it if you didn't write anything yet. All this stuff you've been hearing? It just isn't right."

"I see," she said, looking huffy. "But you've certainly been giving interviews to all the *city* papers. I've read the articles. I bet they pay you. Well, forget you. I don't need this little story."

Feeling sick, he watched as she snatched up her papers, popped out of her chair and left. Didn't even say g'bye.

Whew, A-K thought. Doc's the only one who knows, absolutely knows what happened, 'sides me. If he were here, he'd tell the whole town I didn't do anything to the controls. He's a good pilot; he'd never let a kid, any kid, touch 'em in that kind of weather.

Only trouble was, Doc was gone. He closed down his dental practice last Monday. His friends said the despondent man had bought a ticket for an Alaskan cruise. At this very minute, he was probably sailing up through the Inside Passage on a big Holland-America ship. A-K's "alibi" wasn't going to be back for at least a solid month.

On a gray morning, coming back from the basketball court, A-K threw his smelly gym shoes into his open locker and headed for the showers. By now, he was so used to the sight of the brown jacket stuffed in the back he hardly noticed it anymore.

One time – only once – his father had asked him why he didn't wear his birthday jacket very much, and he'd said, truthfully, "Well, guess I left it at school again." If Viktor Kerzak had some extra thoughts about that, he'd kept them to himself.

Right now, standing under a hot shower with the rest of the guys (most of them weren't talking to him), A-K was trying to invent a truthful-sounding story about why he hadn't finished the Social Studies report that was due, in fifteen minutes.

His teachers had been fairly lenient so far. For a brief while there'd been this "imagine what that young man has been through" phase. But now, he knew from looking at their faces he'd just about used up everybody's good will.

While the Freshman guys were still yelling around in the showers, Mark McCallister suddenly appeared in the empty locker room. He carried a couple of books and his canvas sports bag. Having been in P. E. just before this class, he was cussing at himself right now for forgetting his letterman sweater. He told himself – hurry! That jerk of a Math teacher would probably raise holy hell if he was late again.

The deal was: his sister, Eleanor, had promised to sew on the new varsity letter in exchange for his driving her and some girl friends over to the mall, Saturday. Hurriedly Marko stuffed his bulky sweater into the bag, then started back out. As he passed by the row of open lockers: he thought, *dumb ninth graders, always leavin' their stuff around. Bunch of punks.*

Almost out the door, he suddenly came to a halt. Hey, Kerzak's in this class. Yeah, he's always coming in just when I'm goin' out. Interesting.

Until this minute, Marko'd had no plans for giving A-K any particular grief today. He just had an on-going urge to get back at him for, well, everything. Damn show-off – the creep's story was on TV *again* last weekend.

Heating himself up he thought: Kerzak thinks he's so cool nowdays, just 'cause of the accident. The stocky athlete flipped around, heading back to the Freshman lockers. "Guy jus' makes me want to puke," he muttered.

Now he started cruising along the locker wall. Les'see, he reminded himself, it's in the low three hundreds, I 'member – all the fourth period guys are along here. Rapidly, he yanked open the few lockers in the row that weren't open already.

302? Nope. 300, no, 304, 305 -06? No. -07? This is it!: 308! Yeah, here's a book with the jerk's name on it. So-o, let's jus' see...

Marko's first idea was to throw A-K's street clothes on the wet cement floor. Then, suddenly focusing on the brown jacket way in the back, he flipped around to see if anybody was coming. Still alone in the high-ceilinged room, taking a deep breath, he leaned in and snatched it.

On the inside collar he saw the tag: *Kerzak* carefully sewn on. "Right," Marko muttered, "an' I bet I can think of somethin' real fun to do with it, too."

Hearing voices coming toward him from the shower room, Marko went into action. Unzipping his canvas tote again, he yanked out his own sweater, and shoved A-K's corduroy jacket into the long bag. Couldn't get its zipper closed all the way, but looking down at it, he was satisfied the ninth graders couldn't see anything.

He hustled toward the door, draping his athletic sweater over his arm and waded right into a crowd of the "Fresh Little Men", as he and his friends called them. Glowering, he bulled his way through the whole stupid bunch. And not one person dared complain about the guy's rude shoving.

Mess around with McCallister, people knew, you're headed for trouble.

CHAPTER 20

Marko called out, "Yo, Mr. Groogan!" The football player jammed on the brakes, bringing his jeep right up next to the office-trailer. "Got a minute?"

The manager was kneeling down next to one of his favorite rose bushes – an orange species called "Dancer" – adding more fertilizer from the green cellophane bag next to him. With a slight frown, he glanced at the clouds of dust kicked up by the jeeps speedy arrival.

"Well, yes, I s'pose so. What can I do for you?" Still turning over the caked dirt, he waited for the young man to step out of the car.

Marko didn't. He didn't even bother to open the car door. Instead, he just sat there with the window rolled down, one eyebrow cocked at an angle. Had a look on his face like his patience was going to run out any minute now.

"This a social call, young fella?"

"Nope. I've got some business to talk over with you."

Grogan pushed his trowel into the dirt and heaved himself up. He made an effort to look pleasant.

"Actually, I drove all the way out here, see, 'cause I'm lookin' for a job. And I hear there's gonna be an opening." At the last minute, Marko added "Sir."

He was pretty sure Tina would be impressed with his new job. Also, time to get rid of that foreign guy, thinks he's so hot.

"Is that so?" the manager asked evenly. "Where'd you hear that? And, what kind of work were you thinking of doing, even if there *was* an opening?"

"Well, I can learn prac'ly anything, given some time, you know. For starters, I want to be one of those line boys you got."

"Oh thanks, son, but see, I've got plenty of help in that department, already..."

"Hey, listen, no insult or anything," Marko interrupted loudly, "but look – people are kinda wonderin' about some of the guys you got workin' out here."

"What's that? Say – what are you talking about?"

"Well, the rumor is..." Marko slowed down now, realizing the instructor might not fall for the story as fast as the kids at school had.

"Uh, my dad – he's a long-time pilot himself – he thinks that guy you got workin' out here? That foreign kid, Kerzak? Well, they say he was the one doin' the flyin' when that sailplane smashed up. The one almost got the dentist killed?"

Grogan gave his bulbous nose a quick rub. "Now just wait a minute, here. You've got this all cockeyed..."

"Also," the clueless boy rushed on, "guess you've met my father, Len McCallister? – he's got the Chrysler-Cadillac shop out on Highway 20? Well, he keeps his Mooney right over there in the big hangar. Flies it a whole bunch, so we're a flyin' family, you might say. It's the red one, you know."

Marko swiveled around and pointed to the other end of the field, where the single engine planes were kept, as if maybe Grogan didn't know this. As if he cared.

"So it sort of makes sense to be workin' out here, way I figure it," he added. "Me bein' around planes a lot and folks sayin' you're gonna haf to replace one of the guys..."

Finally, noticing the manager's face still didn't look friendly, the football player added, "*plus*, my dad has, well, ya know, a whole bunch of connections with the FAA."

"Of course I know who your father is," Grogan said briskly. Jamming his hands into his khaki pockets, he peered down at his prize roses as if for comfort.

"Lenny's a fine pilot. Contributes a lot to the community. Don't see much of him, though. My property goes just beyond the grass strip out there. Well, and along that farmer's fence." Grogan waited for that to sink in and then asked, "So, what's your interest in gliders? Never knew you had one."

A little late, Marko realized that getting out of the jeep might be a good move.

"Well, I'm kinda thinkin' of, um, makin' flying my career," he improvised, opening the door. "And to work out here, you know, startin' at the bottom – kinna makes sense."

"The bottom rung? That's what you think gliders are?"

"Naw, I didn't 'zackley mean that. No. But, well – it's a lot easier."

"And how'd you come across that information?"

"I always – well, everybody knows it. Not so many dials and stuff, like in real planes."

"Real planes, huh?" echoed the manager. "Well – let's get back to Andy Kerzak. Listen, young fella, I don't believe he had anything to do with that crash. If he did, Doc Kingsbury would have told me 'fore he left town."

"Oh yeah?" Marko said boldly, " Well, folks are sayin' that's how come the dentist left so fast. And I hear he may not be comin' back, either. Everybody's sayin' it. Felt so bad about it, them bein' friends an all. Older guy, protecting a kid..."

"Hey, that's a bunch of nonsense."

Silence. Then, finally realizing Pat Grogan was not going to give him a job no matter what, Marko said, "Listen, I got plenty of other stuff goin' on. To hell with your little show out here. All these punk guys you got around..."

"That's okay, son. Sorry I can't help you."

Nodding briskly, the heavy-set man turned and headed for the trailer's steps, not aware that he was still clutching his garden trowel. All he could think of now was comforting himself with a mug of strong coffee. – and adding two spoonfulls of sugar to it, nevermind his new diet.

With the trailer door closed behind him, Grogan just shook his head. "What a turkey that kid is. The father seems nice, but..."

Scowling, Marko climbed back into his jeep. As he backed up to leave, he noticed a big Coleman lantern hanging in the door-way of one of the sheds.

Hey, he thought, *now there's an idea...*

"Screw you, Grogan!" he muttered to himself. "Ol' fat slob. I'll fix ya. You and that foreign kid, Kerzak. Whatta name! Kersap is what it oughta be."

He bit down on his lower lip, thinking about the corduroy jacket he'd stolen from A-K's locker. By the time he had gotten back to town, he'd figured out a real sharp plan. "Sure, I can take care of both of ya!" Marko glanced admiringly at the rear-view mirror above him. "Per usual, the ol' brain's jus' speedin' right along here!"

The following Saturday night, while A-K and his two friends were turning in the free passes to the local bowling alley someone had sent him through the mail ("probably some kind of promotion," his dad had groused, "better watch out, Andor, there's always a hitch.") there was also this party starting out at the gliderport.

Four specially chosen guys, each wearing a back pack, had just arrived out there on three motorcycles, rented with one of Marko's false driver's licenses. It was so dark, they could barely see anything.

Dirk Lowinsen who had ridden out with their leader, complained, "Marky, you know me – I'm always up for a li'l party time. But how come we're parkin' down here by this cruddy old trailer? I vote for your dad's hangar. It's been rainin' here. What's the deal with us party-ing in the cold?"

"Yeah! Rained Thursday and Friday – hell, this place's prac'ly a swamp," Joe Wilder chimed in.

With effort, Marko held himself in. No need for these dopes to know his true motives.

"Listen, guys, we're over here because there's usually pilots workin' in the big hangars," he lied. "Even at night. No foolin', they're close to bein' nut cases. Treat their planes better'n their families, some of 'em..."

"Don't see any lights over there," Dirk persisted. "Maybe I'll buzz over an' take a look. Wan' me to?"

"Nah, forget it! For one thing, they don't leave the doors open," Marko said, removing his heavy backpack. "Don' want stuff to blow in, like maybe somebody's paintin' or something. Anyway, ya jerk, if someone's in there, it won't look too good if we show up – right? Drinkin' under age?"

Dirk, who also played football and was in great shape, muttered, "Hey – knock off callin' me a jerk, okay?"

"Chil-drun, childrun," Joe called, in a conciliatory voice, "Bring on the booze, and stop fussin' around, okay? Com'on, what are we waitin' for?"

Just past midnight now, the four boys settled down on the trailer steps and were soon working their way through a second pack of beer. Wilder's cigarette, which had a particularly funny smell, made the energetic boy laugh so hard at his own dirty jokes that he kept falling off the steps.

Three of them were guzzling lukewarm beer as fast as possible. The fourth, still sober, had taken the Coleman lantern from the shed and had a small, mellow light going on the far side of Grogan's trailer.

Marko had it figured: any driver speedin' by couldn't see squat, but his buddies could.

The best thing for Marko had been dragging Kerzak's brown jacket around in the mud a few days ago. Even looking out the window the maid couldn't see anything either, because he'd hosed the thing down way on the other side of the garage.

"O-kay, McCallister," reminded the bleary-eyed Al Sackett, "You said you'd s'plain why we're partyin' out at the gliderport. How come?"

Marko, who'd carefully downed only half of his first beer, jumped to his feet. "*Races* is why!" he cried. "We're gonna have us some good ol' speed races. Winner gets all the rest of the booze as a reward."

"Cut'n us some wheelies?" Sackett groaned. "Hell, McCallister, tha's grammar school stuff. Besides, the ground's real sloshy."

"Yeah? Sounds like you're afraid of losin' buddy boy," Marko said, aiming his flashlight straight at Al's face. "Afraid ya can't hack it?"

That got them moving. Al, determined to be the first contestant, started revving up his motorcycle.

In no time at all, Dirk was attempting to race Al up and down the mushy grass strip. Joe laughed so hard he started to choke. "Wow, this is like trying to ride through choc'late pudding," Dirk sang out. "But I bet I'll win!"

The friends all kept taking turns except Marko, getting more cans of beer out of their parked backpacks when it wasn't their time to race. Even though the boys fake-argued about who was the "winner", none of them seemed to care very much. At least, not at first.

The only serious gripe any of them had was that the field was "kinna wrecked and getting hard to ride out there."

"Exactly! That's part of the deal," their faithful leader called out. "You know, like in those demolition derbys? More mud the better!"

Pretending to be monitoring his friends with his stopwatch, the bulky athlete had to tell them, twice, to quit shouting and cussing so loud. Bad enough, the sound of the motorcyles. By now, two or three cars had sped past them over on the highway side.

Still, it's a real messy night, he figured – all this rain and we're a-ways off the road. He whispered to himself, "So great, these guys're drunk as skunks."

"O-ka-ay," Marko finally called out. "All-y all-y all-in-free."

The last two contestants wobbled in, Joe panting like a race horse while Al Sackett, looking somewhat ill, pushed his motorcycle back over to the start-up line.

"So, who's the winner?" Dirk demanded. Though he'd lost his dinner a while ago, he was almost sober enough to walk a straight line again, and tried to show them.

"Good job, Lowinsen! Gettin' ready for the Tour de France," Marko drawled. Before Dirk had a chance ask what the 'tour duh pans' was, their leader announced firmly, "Lookit, you guys, it was just too damn close to tell. What we gotta do is have a run-off."

All three of the bleary-eyed contestants groaned. Joe Wilder reached down and popped open another beer can, handed it to Dirk and then opened another one for himself.

"Oh, man," Al complained, "I'm about dyin', I'm so tired. You must'a screwed up, McCallister. Lem'me see that fancy stop watch of yours, will ya?"

"It was too close to tell, and I did not screw up ." No smiles now. Suddenly Marko seemed to remember he was a rich man's son, the kid who had his very own jeep and was the "toughest" guy on the second-string football team.

"So now, folks," he announced, all pleasant again, "we're gonna have us one more race, see who's the ab-solute, final winner. This is the one that counts. Not out on the field, anymore – it's all globbed up. This time, you gotta finish by racing right along here, near the trailer. See – between it and that driveway fence."

He studied his friends. Yeah, they were so out of it, they'd do almost anything.

"All ya haf to do is ride those babies straight out to that big madrona, then whip around and get back here, quick as you can. I'll be timin' you – an' the fastest one gets a whole six-pack for himself."

"Hey, it's way too narrow in there," Al protested, squinting at the enclosed area. "That li'l fence is almost next to the trailer. Plus, that stupid garden's in the way. Listen – there isn't enough space for motorcycles."

"Zat's the very challenge," Dirk chimed in loyally. "This'uns harder. Out there, in the fiel', wast easy."

Ignoring his football buddy, Marko whipped around and faced Al. "Listen, Sackett, why don't you take your sissy little butt down the road? G'wan . Get the hell outta of here."

He stared at the wiry boy a full half-minute without blinking. Al made a sudden move as if to jump the taller guy, maybe try to take him apart. In an instant, Marko got into a crouch position, ready for action.

Seeing that, Al hesitated.

"So what's stoppin' you? Huh? Ya chicken? Are you – *chicken?*" Marko taunted, his hands balled-up in tight fists.

Al glanced around to look at the other two and saw, in the shadowy light that no way were his friends going to back him up. "I'm no damn chicken," he muttered. Voice sounded hoarse as if he'd suddenly caught a cold. "But you know where you can go..."

Shaking his head as if getting rid of a mosquito, Marko announced "Okay: two at a time, doesn't matter who's first – grab the 'cycles. Run 'em out, straight down, straight back, then stop."

Whooping it up, Joe and Dirk grabbed up their motorcycles, lined themselves up and, at the shout of *GO*, took off toward the tunnel-like space next to the trailer.

The first of Grogan's rose bushes was smashed by Joe Wilder on his way down. "Ac-cident," he yelled. "But I'm still comin' through!" He roared to the end of the narrow passage, wheeled the heavy machine around and barely missed knocking into Dirk. To avoid getting hit, the taller guy veered into another rose bush, then, over-correcting, smashed into the bottom side of the aluminum trailer leaving a long dent.

Dirk jumped off his motorcycle muttering, "What the hell, McCall'ster, there's not enough room. This place's crudsville!" Joe, panting heavily, rode past him to the finish line.

Marko made a pretense of writing down the "scores" on a little tablet he'd pulled out of his pocket. Mainly, though, he watched the whole scene as if it were a movie. A real squeeze in there. Between 'em, they're about totaling this place. Great.

"Hey – what're the scores now?" Dirk panted.

"Mm?" Pre-occupied, Marko didn't answer right off.

He couldn't remember when he'd felt happier in his entire life, so everything was working out fine. Next couple minutes, after he got these bozos calmed down and back on the rented cycles, he was going to have the extreme pleasure of dumping A-K's fouled-up jacket out there on the grass. It'll be such an interesting calling card!

Stuffed in the canvas bag he'd carried out on his back, the

corduroy coat even had Kerzak's name all neatly sewn in and everything! And that was the name he'd given when they'd rented the motorcycles over in Milltown. In spite of the cold drizzle, the muscular boy smiled. Yep, the whole mess's gonna end up in your lap, A-K, Mr. Ache-in-the-Butt.

"Com'mon, what're the damn scores?" Dirk demanded.

"Dirker, will ya please shud-up a minute? You didn't win, that's for sure." Marko snapped. "It's between Al and Joe Wilder now. Not *you* ."

Joe carefully put his lighted joint down on the trailer's wet step. Al guzzled down the last of his beer, and then they lined up. No more jokes now.

Both boys, neither of them sober, bumped into each other and also zig-zagged into a couple of the remaining rose bushes. Veering off to the right, Al hit and splintered a piece of the lichen-covered fence, cussed a blue streak, but quickly got himself back onto the narrow passage way.

On the way back, Joe, with teeth bared, ran broadside into one end of the trailer again – probably by accident – leaving one more dent in the office's metal wall. That didn't stop him more than a few seconds, though. Fueled by marijuana, beer and fury, the boy backed up, re-aimed himself, and then shot forward.

"All *right*, " shouted Marko, as Joe skidded across the muddy line. "Wilder won out in the field, an' Wilder's won back here, too." Although Al had passed out by now, Dirk cheered hoarsely.

"Tee-rific! And congrat-u-lations to..." All of a sudden, Marky McCallister shut right up.

A cop car had just driven in. First, seen through the rain with its low lights. Then – no lights.

For a moment, Marko's mind went blank; he just stood there, frozen, staring at the squad car. Then, breathing through his pursed mouth, he began to wonder what his parents were going to do to him (if you are a McCallister, can you buy your way out of Juvvie?). His next thought was: After all my work, that bugger's gonna find Kerzak's jacket in my backpack. Oh crap, I think I'm screwed.

Military school down in Portland., that's what Dad had warned, "if there's one more incident." Neb'mind, Juvvie.

That was "little Marky" all over, just as his grandma always said, "quick as a wink." Fortunately, the last two contestants, not to mention the third who was still zonked out, didn't understand there was a squad car in their midst.

Not right away.

But, how could they have known? The black and white car had purred in so silently. The lights were snuffed off. In fact, both of the remaining contestants were still full of smiles, waiting for their leader to tell them how great they were.

The Irish cop hadn't stepped into the arena yet. The racers just didn't *realize*.

But they tuned right in when the policeman, out on his regular beat, turned his high beams back on. And in case that hadn't warned them, there was also the loud sound of a squad car door being slammed hard behind this huge and very serious-lookin' cop: Police Officer Shawn Joseph Mulroney.

CHAPTER 21

S ometimes A-K felt as if he were going bonkers. Over and over in his mind, he kept trying to figure out what had happened up there. Had he really grabbed hold of the metal stick when that weather got so rough? Or, unaware, had he stepped on one of the rudders, sending them spiraling down?

He kept asking himself: *Was it my fault? Did I make the wreck?* His dreams were even worse...

Marko had put out all kinds of bad stuff about him, before he got sent away. "Oh yeah, that Kerzak kid made the plane crash, all right. I got the real information. Guy jus' won't admit it."

A-K hoped at least some of them hadn't made up their minds yet, least not until he'd gotten it straight, himself. But he was learning new things: Some people liked hearing how someone else had screwed up. It made them feel better about themselves.

Even though McCallister was down at that military school in Oregon now, he'd sure left a whole bunch of trouble behind for A-K.

It wasn't any secret in St. Clair, a town of only thirteen hundred and forty people according to the last census, that most people admired the successful McCallisters.

So, in spite of the 'little beer party' out at the airfield a few weeks ago, the feeling was that boys will be boys. It was just kids "sowing their oats" once in a while.

After all, young Mark came from such a nice, and generous, family. Why, they'd contribute to almost any cause you asked for.

Two years ago, for instance, Mr. McCallister had put up every single bit of the money for those night lights at the baseball field! The only pay back, as he modestly called it, was that his company's name be put on every other billboard that surrounded the field. His energetic wife, Darlene, ran the yearly Red Cross drive. They were pillars of their church and major donors to the town's little theater, not to mention the nailed-up brass plaques all over town with the name McCallister on them, from the park benches they'd paid for, to the Medical Center's new trees. Good heavens, they were the backbone of the community!

About their questionable son, they said: "Well, we're thinking about sending him to Harvard later, so we thought it was a good idea to get him used to a prep school, first."

"Hey there, Tina," A-K kept trying, in the hallways.

"Oh, hul-lo," she'd say in a downhill voice, then glance down at her notebooks. She looked more baffled than mad.

He figured it wasn't about the actual collision, exactly. She'd probably realize, even if it *had* been his fault, that anybody can make a mistake. Her pilot brother must have talked about flying in bad weather.

Naw, it probably wasn't that. Bet she'd quit on him because A-K wouldn't admit what he'd "done."

Well, he couldn't. Because he hadn't.

At his lowest ebb—and this was the scariest thing of all— once in a while he almost believed the town's version of the crash. He wondered if maybe he'd blanked out for a minute and really did something awful up there, by accident.

And, if he had, then that would explain why Doc had taken off for Alaska. God A'mighty – tryin' to protect "the Kerzak kid".

He let that sizzle around in his mind for several minutes. Then decided: NO! I was totally scared to touch any of those instruments. I gotta hang on to what I know, and not let this town psych me out.

Much of the time now, A-K did things alone. Even though his two buddies still saved him a seat in the cafeteria, it seemed like both of them kept having all this "stuff to do" after school, and usually didn't ask him to come along. Stoically, he pretended he was extra busy, himself.

Who needs friends like them anyway, he kept telling himself, guys who'll drop you fast if you get in trouble? Back in Arizona, you're a buddy or you're not. The ones out here – hah!

But when classes were out, he didn't want to just go home to an empty house, either. Being stuck with only his own thoughts was too depressing, even with the TV and radio going at the same time.

A-K felt he couldn't go out to the gliderport either; no telling what the boss thought about him now. So, as a last resort, he started hanging out at the cleaners.

He got to thinking, for maybe the first time, that he was lucky to even *have* parents. Dad had lost his by the age of twelve. His growin' up must of been even more lonely than this.

In fact, the folks did have some good points: them givin' him a place to live, clothes, and totally backing him on this mess right down the line.

He was having a change of heart, sort of like his father'd had with that operation. Just thinking the goofy connection made A-K smile and he repeated it outloud. A change of heart – yep, that's it!

To help fill his free time, A-K figured out a job that the folks hadn't even thought of: he started delivering stuff by hand. After school, a couple of times a week, he carried boxed shirts and cellophaned uniforms to some of the merchants who worked on Main Street. He found out he liked being around the hard-working folks who didn't have much time, or inclination, for gossip.

And they seemed to be impressed that an actual teenager would take the time to talk to them, one who didn't treat them like ol' fogeys.

"That Andy Kerzak— why he's just a nice, regular kid," the merchants started saying to each other. "Bet'cha anything he didn't knock that plane out of the sky. It was the storm."

"I like that boy of yours," crusty old Phil Daugherty from the gift shop told Illona Kerzak, "he's got some decent manners— for a young person"

"Hey that's a first !" A-K said, when his mother told him.

Another one, the bakery lady, whose name he still couldn't pronounce, had started giving him a pancake-sized cookie everytime he brought back one of her newly starched uniforms. Through their Main Street windows, tradespeople smiled as they saw the short boy hustle up and down the sidewalks, returning their cellophaned clothes.

Without realizing it, he was turning into a walking advertisement for his folks: Hey, have you noticed, please? A new family's come to town: the Kerzaks. And like you, we work hard, pay our taxes, and have our own dreams, too.

"I haven't seen much of Heck, nowadays. You aren't mad at each other, are you?" his mother asked him late one afternoon. "And that other fellow, Bop? Did I get the name right?"

"Uh huh. I mean, no! It's *Boz*." Ordinarily, that riff on his friend's name would have made him prac'ly fall over laughing. Nowdays, though, he didn't have much of a laugh in him.

"Naw, I'm doin' okay. Just tryin' to—get by."

"Well, that's good," she said, wiping off the shop's formica counter one more time than it needed, "It's, well—I hate to see you being so... serious. Don't forget your friends."

"Hey, Mo-ther—I'm almost fifteen, okay? Things're goin' great." Oh sure.

Finally, around the middle of May, A-K found something that really turned him on. Mr. Hanssen, the white-bearded shop teacher, informed his class that each student was to start making plans for their end-of-semester project. He told them that if they wanted, he would help each of them create something "useful" out of wood. Size didn't matter.

"Workmanship, that's what I'll be looking for." Curtly, he told them to give it some thought as most of the semester's grade for each of the thirteen boys and two girls depended on their final product.

At first, A-K figured he'd make another bread board, give it to ol' Phoebe, maybe for "Sister-in-law" day if there was such a thing. Seemed she'd been improving a little since the crash, wasn't laying all this "helpful" advice on him the way she used to.

Then, as he rode home from school several days later, he suddenly knew just what he wanted to make.

Chancing on a fine piece of walnut in the shop's barrel of scraps, A-K set to work the next day. This time he used the jigsaw with much greater care than before. He carved out a wooden heart about the size of a Ritz cracker. After a few days, Mr. Hanssen wandered over to his work table and inspected the piece the Kerzak boy was working on.

"Didn't know I had any fine wood left in there," the old teacher said gruffly. "Humph, yes. Nice, what you're making. So how're you going to finish it?"

"I dunno, sir, exactly. But see, I was thinkin' of first sanding it off real good. Then, might paint some little designs on it? Colored ones? And, at the end, finish it off with a layer or two of shellac. That sound okay?"

He was remembering some of the delicate motifs his grandparents had painted on their wooden Christmas present ornaments sent from Switzerland.

"I see, yes. And then what?"

"Well," A-K swallowed. "Like – drill a hole in it, in the heart's 'v', right here? And maybe someone could – um," he shrugged. "Well, she could wear it - on a chain? If she wanted to."

"Yes, that's a good idea," Mr. Hanssen said, matter-of-factly. "But I'd suggest, besides drilling the hole, you buy a little gold circle from the jewelers. It shouldn't cost more than a couple of dollars, and have them connect it through the hole. With a chain through that, your little piece will lay smooth."

The tough old teacher even smiled. "Go ahead, yes," he rumbled. "You'll make somebody happy."

From time to time, Heck came over from the next table to see how the project was coming along.

"Hey, you gotta sand those edges better," his bushy-haired friend advised as he was just leaving class on this particular Thursday. Heck pointed to one of the sides. "Ya want it to feel like glass, 'fore you seal it up."

A-K nodded, seriously. "You're right, man!" he said. After that, he made himself slow *way* down.

It took four more days—including putting on the last layer of shellac—for the piece to completely dry. Then, when he was satisfied the little heart looked totally fine – and when the curt old teacher agreed – A-K boxed it in soft cotton, and sent it through the mail to Miss Tina Beckman.

He just up and sent it, without any return name or address from the sender.

There was one other special event happening this month, or anyway A-K thought it was a big deal: on the last day of a very long month, the word was out that Dr. Kingsbury was back.

CHAPTER 22

A-K him found at the drugstore, of all places. *"Doc!"* he hollered racing down the main aisle, and skirting six or seven people in the way. "When'd you get back?"

"Hey – hi-ya, kid! Jus' the guy I wanna see! Got back yesterday. Well... actually, last night."

To get closer, the boisterous man hustled himself around an end counter that held ladies' stockings on sale. "Was gettin' ready to call ya up, bud, soon's I got my allergy medicine refilled. So how you been?"

Before A-K even had a chance to open his mouth and yell "Terrible, thats how!" Doc placed his big hands on the boy's shoulders. "Jus' wait'll ya see all the stuff I bought you in this fantastic store up in Skagway. Not to mention, you just cannot believe the scenery..."

"No!" A-K cried. He ducked out of Doc's grip. "I don' care about presents. Jus' leg-go. I don't even wanna listen to you. You don't know how bad it's been round here. People sayin' I made the crash, sayin' how poor you prac'ly got killed – because of *me.*"

The more he talked, the madder he got. "Yeah, you and your big vacation. I was down here takin' all the flak. Thanks a lot! My parents losing customers, an' kids at school treatin' me like I got leprosy."

Never in his whole life had A-K talked this way to a grownup before, but then never had he felt so persecuted before, either.

"Hey – slow down, Andy. Great Scott. I can't believe what you're telling me. This's terrible!" Doc's face showed concern, but A-K was sure he couldn't know how terrible.

"Sounds like the facts got all balled up, doesn't it," the dentist said slowly. "But still – maybe you're bein' over-touchy? I just can't believe anybody thinks..."

"Doc? You don't understand! You been gone!"

Hearing the commotion, several more people stuck their heads around the aisle. One, an elderly woman (and a noted gossip) rounded the corner and inched toward them, pretending she was fascinated by the baby diapers display.

"See, I gotta get this straightened out. Right now! Tell me the truth, Doc: before we crashed, do you think I could've – accidentally – worked the rudders in back? And that's what brought us down? I'm almost sure I didn't touch the stick, but anyway, how 'bout the rudders?"

"No, of course not. I was working the rudders up front, an' I've got a heavy foot. It's a bunch of bull, whatever someone might'a told you. *I* ran that expedition all by myself. Naw, it was that bastard of a wind got us, kid. Worse storm I've ever been in. Lordy, I should'a called you from Alaska... sure thought about it, but – ended up figuring you had such a nice big family down there, you'd be okay. We'd connect, when I got back."

Frowning, Doc Kingsbury shook his head. "I never thought anybody'd try and pin it on *you*, kid. That's so stupid. A-ahh! Sounds like you been havin' to take all the heat for both of us."

A-K squinched his eyelids together, as if there were gnats suddenly dive-bombing his face. "Well – nobody can stop it now," he muttered. "It was mainly that Marko, an' he's gone now; got sent down to Portland for school, but the stuff he spread before he left – it's still got people all flummoxed. He told everybody that I made the wreck, as if he knew anything."

He hesitated for a minute, then added, "Also, my main friends're —embarrassed to even hang out with me now, 'specially in public."

"The power of gossip," Doc whispered to himself. Pursing his mouth, he stood completely still for about a minute. Then, with no warning, the tall bald man roared into action.

He shouted straight up toward the drugstore's high ceiling: *"Hey folks, it's me - Doc Kingsbury, back home again. Listen up! The storm last month? It knocked my plane down, and this punk kid standing right here? This Andy Kerzak – he saved my life!"*

Then he bowed to Andy, the old fashioned way: with one arm crossed in front over his waist, and the other arm stretched over his belt line in the back.

Nobody in the entire drugstore said a word. All you could hear was the huge round clock over the pharmacist's counter sounding a click as each full minute went by.

Highly embarrassed, A-K glanced around. It was like the game of Stop and Go. Everybody in the store was frozen on STOP!

A-K shifted from one foot to the other. Then he stole another look at the dentist. "Hey," he smiled, when he finally got hold of his voice again, "sure glad you're back. Feels like – well, it's been a long time, sir. So, c'mon, where're all these fancy presents you brought me?"

Three weeks later, when school was finally out and the country was beginning to smell like summer, A-K got a chance to take even another glider lesson with Grogan. Doc was paying; he'd told Grogan just to keep a running tab.

It began as just a routine flight. Things were going along pretty well until, at eight hundred feet, with Ron towing in the Super Cub, up ahead, the unthinkable happened. A-K heard the sudden bang of the hook. Somehow, he'd released too early.

"Uh oh – we're in trouble son! Flyin' too low," Grogan growled from the back. "Whatta ya gonna do 'bout it?"

Automatically, A-K lowered the glider's nose to maintain flying speed. With a dry mouth and heart thumping every which way, he entered a close-in pattern. The ground was coming up fast, fields and fences flashed by at odd angles like car racing video games. Sitting bolt upright, he improvised a pattern and lined up on final approach, telling himself: set the spoilers and I should make it.

They touched down hard, bounced twice, sped across the grass runway, slowed, slow-ed, then came to a full stop. Gently, the yellow glider tipped over to one side. Grogan popped open the canopy but didn't say anything. Not at first.

Oh man, A-K thought, how come I did so bad? What'd I do this time? Release from the rope too soon? Screw up with the spoilers?

The last thing he expected was to have the instructor break into a rumbling chuckle. "Fan-tastic!" Grogan announced. Loosing himself from the harness, A-K lurched around to stare at the burly instructor.

"See, Andy, *I* unhooked us from tow. Do it at least once to all my students, see how they handle it. Y'know, to make an emergency landing. You did great!"

Grogan reached forward and thunked him hard on the shoulder. "All right, son – you want to try it alone this time?"

"You mean like, today? *Solo?*"

"Yep. You've had, what – eleven, twelve flights since Doc's been back? Must add up to nearly twenty by now, if we count this one."

"Well, yes, but a lot of 'em were just like, um, flyin' over the field – ten or fifteen minutes worth. Those count?"

"Sure they do. You've been doing most of your own landings this month and the last few were good ones.

Grogan stretched both his shoulders, one at a time. "Remember, he continued, you can't get a license until you're sixteen, but I think you're ready to try it now by yourself."

A-K looked down at his fisted hands a second, then peered out through the curved plexiglass. Heck was staring over at them – or at least looking their way. Seemed like his friend's broad face was kinna tight. Would Judson be mad if he soloed first? Maybe. The guy got out here first, that's for sure.

No way did he want to lose a friend. Still, Heckle hadn't been around much lately. Skiing all winter and, well, he calls himself a jack of all trades. Also, his dad's teachin' him to drive already..."

"Okay, Mr. Grogan, yes. Just lemme get a drink out of my thermos if you don't mind." Gulping down the lukewarm water, A-K remembered the dozens of times he'd thought of what solo would be like – how he'd planned it out in bed, not sleeping; day-dreaming in class, not listening.

Wonder if I should call the folks, he thought. Naw, they're gettin' swamped with all the new business comin' in. I don't think they'd have the time. Anyway, Heck's usin' the phone right now. Also, if I saw Dad down there pacing around, for sure it'd wreck my concentration. Better tell him later, if I've pulled it off.

"I'm ready, sir," he said. The ever-patient Grogan climbed out of the back of the glider. He had a secret little smile on his face like something nice was about to happen.

Gearing up mentally, A-K told himself: now *just do it*. Don't think too much. Time to get this show on the road.

After a quick call from Grogan's hand-held phone, Ronvold taxied the red and white plane up close to the glider. Hook-up, last minute instructions, safety belt snapped back on, harness fastened, canopy down and secured.

Grogan himself ran the wing tip for A-K—this, the man who'd let him know he could do things right, even if he wasn't a grown up yet..

A-K sucked in his breath. Oh man oh God, please: I don' wanta mess this up. Let me do it right. I—oh YES, here-we-go!

Next thing he knew, the yellow Schweizer was jolting down the runway behind Ron. The wide-winged ship lifted off the ground before the powered Super Cub did up in front.

Too early?

A second later he scolded himself: Hey, get it together, Kerzak, okay ? It's what's s'posed to happen. I'm flying the lighter ship. Also, there's only one person in here now – me!

Con-cen-trate: Don't want to let this baby get up too high. Ten feet above the towplane. No more.

Ron had them turning now, climbing up—and up—finally leaving the pattern. Glancing at the fancy watch Doc had given him, A-K saw that they were only seven minutes out. The glider's altimeter read 1,000 feet. The safety of the farmer's straw-colored pastures was way behind them. The two planes, still attached, headed for the low-lying green hills.

Swallowing in a dry throat A-K, pinned his eyes on the altimeter. Climbing up and up and up – 2,000 – 2,400 – now, *3,000 feet.* After hesitating a heart-pounding minute, he forced himself to pull out the red knob. He heard the familiar bang saw the towplane dive off and away, its snake-like rope whipping back and forth as it headed down towards the safety of the airport.

And, here was something wonderful: right now, he wasn't – very scared.

Instead, as soon as he was on his own, A-K began pretending he was riding this plane bareback, ghosting through the sky. No sound, no fuss. He had this crazy-wild urge to holler: *Hey world. I'm up here! Me, Andor Kerzak, and I'm doin' it!*

The elation didn't last all that long, though. Now, working the stick, A-K abruptly thought: people get killed in planes all the time. Not just in wars, every single day people're crashin' all over the place!

His heart began ticking extra fast, but after a few nervous minutes he told himself: would you please stop looking for trouble? Just fly the dang thing.

Briefly relaxed, he snatched a quick look-around. Inhaled some calm from the soft sky: bleached-blue and cloudless.

He popped out of his near-trance when he heard a brand new sound. Never heard that noise before. Oh geez, the elevator's falling off...

Half a minute later: No, it's not, Kerzak. Just cool it.

Any planes headin' this way? Don't see any. *So* – how far can I fly from the field and still get back? What do the guys call it? Leavin' the nest? Well, looks like there's some good lift over Cougar Mountain, lotta birds circling around. Should I go for it?

Naw, not this time. No sense tryin' to be a hero. Keep it simple, re-tard. He checked over his shoulder. Yeah, s'okay, St. Clair's still back there.

Ahh ha! – and what do we have down there? Well, well! The dis-gusting town of Milltown. Maybe time to wipe out our com-petition: Get ready, you dirty ol' cleaners. All the time tryin' to beat out my folks. Guess I'm gonna haf-ta strafe – hey Kerzak! Quit daydreaming, will ya? Gonna lose the updraft.

Sweating, but a little more confident now, he flew straight

and level, banked sideways for the turn, straightened out, and finally whisked the glider over his own town at 1,800 feet. Man, the place looks small. Good trees down there, a bunch of good people, too.

Lem'me see if I can find Tina's house. That might be it straight down there – it's her neighborhood, anyway. Little fire station's where you turn left. How 'bout I try and just dust off her roof, yell down somethin' real casual, like: hi babe, just passin' by and I'm wonderin' will you be my girlfriend?

Hey, get it together, man. 'Bout time to take this bird down now. Been up here—wow!— twenty-eight minutes already. Long enough.

Closer to the field just ahead, he planned his approach. So, check the windsock: breeze's coming out from the southeast. Good! Lucky not to have a crosswind down there: that'd make it way harder to land. Guess Grogan checked the weather report this morning, too.

Okay, here we go: down and... around, and down... lookin' good, lookin' *good*...

Then he smiled, realizing he was telling himself the same stuff that the instructor called up from the back seat, when things were going right. Grogan's best praise was "Lookin' good."

Below: no traffic in sight. Field looks quiet.

Back in the pattern again, his breathing slowed down to almost normal. Cool, he thought, way that 172 looks down by the hangar. Like a little badge pinned on the grass. Hah, I shoulda been a poet. So now, let's do this right – downwind, open spoilers, turn to left base – yes, then straight in, on final. Yes!

The glider whistled right over the farmer's fence. Touched down, bumped up once more, hit down bumpty thump-bump, then rolled out ni-ice and smooth. Came to a complete – stop. Gently, the motor-less plane rolled over to one side, touching the mowed grass with a long yellow wing.

Okay, so I overshot the turn to final at the end there, an' hadda put on some extra rudder to put myself in line with the runway. But it's okay, he thought. Other guys hav'ta do it sometimes, too.

It's legal.

As he rested his head back on the seat, A-K whispered, "Did it right this time...I know I did."

The crew—Grogan's loyal flock—came hurrying over to him. The red-headed boss first, his round, freckled face all crinkled up with smiles. Then Heckle, carrying a big pair of desk scissors. A smiling Ron, with his cowboy hat, right behind them.

Beyond them: Whoa, I can't believe it! As he unlatched the glass canopy, A-K thought he saw Miz Tina Beckman over there parking her bike.

Lightly, he stepped out onto the beautiful, solid, wonderful, earth again. He sneaked another look, then decided, yep, it's her all right. Did she ride all the way out here just to see...well, probably not. A coincidence?

Hurrying toward his friends, he wondered if maybe Heckle had told her. Maybe that's what the nutcase was doin' on the phone? But why'd she come? Tina doesn't like me anymore.

Then he remembered: Of course, she's here to fill up the school paper. Must be hard up for news.

True to solo custom, Ron snipped A-K's thin T-shirt off eight inches from the bottom hem. Grogan stood around grinning like a freckled Halloween pumpkin. Heck offered insulting congratulations.

"Hey, listen you guys," A-K protested in a burst of happiness – "this is the shirt I go to the opera in! You're *wrecking* it." Part of him was still airborne, sailing a plane that flashed light off the sun.

Now, back down safe on earth again, he laughed louder than all of them, groaning at the jokes that were being tossed at him. Out of the corner of his eye, though, he kept his eye on Tina, trying to figure out what she was up to.

Jus' look at her, he thought, trying not to. Still standing over there by her bike. Never thought of her bein' shy. Wonder if she knows who sent the heart? S'pose she still thinks I wrecked the... naw. Probably not anymore. Doc's been talking all over town the last few weeks.

Maybe 'cause of Ron? Half the women out here fall in love with him, seems like...

Heck kept hovering around the crew. "Ya know," he announced importantly, "I'm gonna get goin' on my solo, too. Trouble is, seems like I always got so much other stuff to do..."

"Ah, young Hector, never change," Ron said. "You're lovable, just the way you are."

"Yeah, keep hearing that from others, too," Heck retorted. "All these women jus' keep chasin' me around. Gets me so tired... see, that's my main problem – I'm worn out."

Bunched up with them, not saying much, Grogan laughed at the jokes. Smiling, with his thick fingers folded behind his head, he stood there, protective, as if this were his own little family.

"Hey, young lady," Grogan suddenly called out, looking toward the bike rack. "C'mon over. You gotta congratulate our brand new pilot. He's been working pretty hard for this ride."

Okay now, A-K cautioned himself, she just wants somethin' to write for the school paper, probably a two-inch article. Solo's not that big a deal, so don't get a swelled-up head.

When Tina finally came up close, though, he caught his breath. Oh m'god, she's wearing the little heart I made in woodshop. Huh! Does she know who made it?

The group's circle opened up to include the determined girl. "Nice to have another of Andy's friends out here today," Grogan said in an uncle-y kind of voice. "So – *Heckle!* Come on over to the office with me, will you? Help me figure out when the next lesson's coming up. Oh, and I'll get your logbook for you, son. We've got to get it signed off."

Hector clearly did not want to leave, but the lanky boy trailed along after the boss. Ronvold, claiming he had to move the Super Cub, also disappeared.

"Listen, you didn't tell them I'm your girlfriend or anything, did you?" Tina demanded, the minute the others were gone.

"No, uh uh, I promise! I never said that to anybody. Not one single time." Geez, he thought, she even talks martial arts. "But look, I know you only came out here for the paper, but lemme talk first. Okay?"

She wrapped her arms around herself and stuck her chin out. "Sure, be my guest."

Man, he thought, karate's wreckin' the women of today. "Listen, Tina, I'm not the one that messed up the field that night. You know that?"

"I know it. Everybody does. So why're you telling me?"

"Jus' tryin' to get in good with you. You know I also didn't wreck Doc's plane, right?"

Her high, cheek-boned face colored. "Yes," she said. "And... I wasn't being a very good friend, was I, to think that dumb rumor might be true. One of the main reasons I came out – well, I need to tell you, I'm really... sorry."

Lowering her head, she took hold of the little heart A-K had tried to make so nice. After a minute she let it fall back against her green sweater. "It's so – special," she murmured. "Came from you, didn't it?"

"Right, and now you really owe me, right?"

"You said that two times in one sentence, Andor."

"Uh, right... " he repeated trying to make a joke out of it. This was the longest conversation he'd ever had with a girl. He'd about run out things to say.

Maybe just to help him out, Tina reached out with both hands, smiling, and pulled his face closer. She kissed him right on the mouth, in front of all the gliders and the crew and the birds and the cows and all the cars and the trucks zooming by. Kissed him, it felt like, in front of the whole fantastic, beautiful world.

Holy Toledo, I can't believe this, A-K thought, backing away to catch his breath. He was so happy, he suddenly felt like yelling his fool head off. At the rate his chest was pounding, he wondered if she could hear it. "Oh, *my*," he said, stepping back. "Whoa! Karate babes are sure – aggressive! Listen, we better discuss this some more, if you got any free time."

"I have free time. And I want you to know I admire you for helping out your folks, the way you do. And also, for earning these lessons by yourself."

Impulsively, he reached out to touch her again. However, out of the corner of his eye he saw Grogan and Heck marching toward them. The instructor was holding A-K's log book.

Great! Time to sign off, just like a regular pilot.

Up close, Heck, looking back and forth, checked out both his friends. After giving each of them an unblinking stare, and apparently figuring out they weren't going to run off and get married just yet, the curly-haired boy took a huge, exaggerated stretch, as if he were the star of some movie.

"Hey, An-the-Man," he asked joyfully, "wanna know what a butterfly is? Tina, I know you're smarter, but don't tell 'im."

"A what? A *butterfly*? What are you talkin' about, dork?"

He flipped a look at Tina, then frowned at his friend's wide, show-off grin.

"Don't try to figure it out, man. It's gonna be too hard for your li'l pea brain. So lemme tell ya, okay?" Obviously pleased with himself, Heck started jogging in place.

"Here it comes!" A-K rolled his eyes. "G'wan. Let's have it."

"A butter-fly," Heck pronounced, still jogging, "is a *worm —* that has sprouted wings."

"Is that right?" A-K muttered, irritated that Heck was showing off in front of his almost-girlfriend. "Listen, Hucklebird, you callin' me a worm?" He tried to make it sound like a joke, but the truth was, he felt like punching his friend in the mouth.

"Andy-dor, you name it, you-claim-it!"

Laughing, Tina reached out and grabbed hold of A-K's hand, as if they'd always stood around, holding on to each other. Pleased that she'd admired his joke, Heck chose not to notice they were acting kind of lovey-dovey.

Instead, he produced a grin so wide that A-K thought the show-off's face was gonna crack right open.

Pat Grogan, who knew the entire Kerzak family by now — reacted to this last exchange. "Wa-ait a minute, A-K, Andor, Andy, whatever you're callin' yourself lately," he said, stepping forward. "What your good friend is trying to tell you, in his own peculiar way, is: son, you've just turned into — a *flier!*"

GLOSSARY

aileron: a control surface on each wing that allows the pilot to bank or turn the airplane or glider.

elevator: the control surface on the horizontal tail of an aircraft which helps to control the altitude of the aircraft.

fuselage: the body of the aircraft.

lenticular: a long, linear "spaceship" type cloud associated with high winds at high altitude.

pattern: an agreed-upon set of rules for altitudes and directions to fly for aircraft landing and taking off from an airport.

propwash: the disturbance of air caused by an airplanes /propeller which trails behind the airplane.

rate-of-climb: the speed with which an airplane climbs in terms of number of feet per minute.

rotor: the violent movement of air, sometimes marked by a "rotor cloud," which often occurs below and downwind from a lenticular cloud.

rudder: a control surface on the vertical tail of an aircraft that allows a pilot to make a turn of an aircraft by coordinating aileron and rudder control

spoilers: outer surface on the top side of the wing which can be moved around from the inside by the pilot, to create to create increased drag (resistance) and slow the glider down as it prepares to land.

<u>**stick:**</u> a control stick in the cockpit of an airplane or glider by which the pilot can move the ailerons of the wings and elevators of the tail to guide the aircraft in direction and altitude.

<u>**variometer:**</u> an instrument in a glider's cockpit which is so sensitive to atmospheric pressure that it helps the glider pilot if he/she is in lift (rising air) or sink (descending air).

<u>**wave lift:**</u> very fast rising air over a mountain ridge; when winds on the upwind side force a glider/sailplane up and over mountains; the plane, in "wave" can climb to extremely high altitudes, almost as in an elevator.

www.ingramcontent.com/pod-product-compliance
Lightning Source LLC
Chambersburg PA
CBHW022211050726

47590CB00002B/740